BOOKS BY ADÈLE GERAS

The Girls in the Velvet Frame
Other Echoes
Apricots at Midnight

APRICOTS AT MIDNIGHT

ADÈLE GERAS

APRICOTS AT MIDNIGHT

and Other Stories

From a Patchwork Quilt

Illustrated

by Doreen Caldwell

ATHENEUM   1982   NEW YORK

for Linda Jennings

Library of Congress Cataloging in Publication Data
Geras, Adèle.
Apricots at midnight.

Summary: An elderly London dressmaker entertains
a young relative with memories of the world of her youth,
evoked by the scraps from elegant dresses that
she has sewn into a patchwork quilt.
[1. London (England) — Fiction. 2. Dressmaking —
Fiction. 3. Quilting — Fiction] I. Title.
PZ7.G29354Ap   [Fic.]   82-1728
ISBN 0-689-30921-X   AACR2

CONTENTS

Aunt Pinny

HER REAL NAME was Penelope Sophia Pintle, but she had been called Pinny all her life. To me, she was Aunt Pinny, even though I was not a real niece, but the daughter of her cousin, Laura. She was born in London in 1904. Her father, a fairly prosperous civil servant, had died soon after she was born. Their comfortable, pleasant life changed almost overnight, as Mrs Pintle struggled to make some money, fought to maintain at least the appearance of her former wealth. She began to work as a private dressmaker, and became a very successful one in the end, but in those days, they were poor.

Almost the only toys in their house were strands and skeins of silk, like shining butterflies' wings, strange twists of buttons, rustling leaves of tissue paper, and drifts of snippets and clippings from a thousand materials whose names were like a song. There were bits of bombazine and brocade and broadcloth; slivers of slippery silk, slub satin and sarsenet; crumplings of cashmere and cotton; trimmings of taffeta; leftovers of linen and lace, and lawn: a name like a green field full of daisies when you said it. Pinny loved them all.

She, too, became a dressmaker, like her mother. My parents were often abroad during the school holidays, and sometimes I used to stay with her. The house was in a square, tucked behind Kensington High Street, and turning the corner into that square was like stepping

9

back into another time. Even the traffic in the High Street was only a hum in the distance. The houses stood in pairs. Each house had three steps going up to the front door, and fat, creamy-yellow columns on either side of the porch. Many of the doors had rows of little buttons with name-cards beside them. The houses had been turned into bed-sitting rooms, for the most part, but Aunt Pinny lived all alone in hers. People tried to persuade her that she was lonely, but she smiled at them, and told them politely about her many friends. They said she would become bored with her own company, and she would reply: "I've got to know myself well during the last nearly seventy years, and I find myself tolerably interesting. You would be surprised at the entertaining things I can still tell myself. And besides, there is the television in my bedroom. I do enjoy a late-night spine-chiller!" They told her she would become old and helpless. They painted horrible pictures of milk bottles lined up outside the door and herself inside, sick and feeble. "Fiddlesticks!" Aunt Pinny would say. "That's a long way off yet. I'm not even seventy and that's young, nowadays. I'm far from being helpless, as you can see."

It was true. She was neat, and small, and smooth and brown. Her hair was brown, done up in a plump bun at the back. She wore brown or grey skirts, with sharp pleats and straight hems, and blouses with cardigans that never looked baggy. She put a flowered overall on to work in. Her face was long and gentle, like a pretty horse, and her mouth seemed to fall into a smile all by itself, even when Aunt Pinny was not intending to smile at all. She wore a tape measure round her neck, and the front of her overall was stuck with shoals of little silvery pins, like fish. Before I knew her real name, I thought she was called Pinny because of these pins.

Staying with her was the greatest pleasure of my life at that time.

She was always the same person: she did not have a special voice that she used for talking to children. As soon as I stepped into the hall, I became a guest. I had my own little room at the top of the house. There, on the chest-of-drawers, was a sepia photograph in a silver frame, of Aunt Pinny when she was nine. In the photograph, she was standing tidily next to a potted plant, looking at something far away with big, dark eyes under thin eyebrows. She was wearing a white pinafore over a full-skirted dress, and black, flat shoes. Round her neck, there was a chain with a locket hanging from it. Her hair was wavy and dark to the shoulders, with a ribbon tied round it. I used to look at this photograph and think how little she had changed.

When I was at Aunt Pinny's, I stayed up for dinner in the evening, and shared her coffee afterwards. I, too, had a small, gold-rimmed cup, so that it did not matter that my coffee was nearly all milk. Naturally, Aunt Pinny put a stop to her guests carving their initials on the table, or splashing paint all over the carpet, or climbing on to the fire escape at the back of the house. I suppose she knew how to be angry, but I never found anything to do that was naughty enough to make her lose her temper. I never even wanted to try.

We did exciting things together. Once, she took me to Covent Garden market at four o'clock in the morning, to see the lorries loading up with vegetables and fruit. Twice a week we went to the cinema, to a cowboy film if Aunt Pinny could find one, and there was no nonsense about ice-cream spoiling my appetite for tea. At the theatre, Aunt Pinny always knew the wardrobe mistress or the person who helped to dress the star, and we often went backstage to the dressing-rooms after the show. We went everywhere: to auction sales, and puppet shows, and street markets and parks. And, of course, every night I went to bed. Going to bed was the best part of the day, because of the magic patchwork quilt.

There were no flowers on it which came to life, it did not make you invisible, and certainly it never performed any useful kind of magic, like whisking you off to the furthest star in the sky, or granting your dearest wish. Nevertheless, it was enchanted, and I loved to lie in the high, narrow bed, listening to Aunt Pinny's voice unroll the magic of the patchwork, as it covered me from my chin, down a long way past my toes and right off the bed.

Aunt Pinny had started making it as soon as she was old enough to hold a needle. Every little six-sided shape had a story to go with it, and all through her life, Aunt Pinny had added more patches and more stories. The quilt was an endless pattern, coloured all the colours in the world: all the flowers, all the rainbows, all the days and nights. Each night, when I was in bed, Aunt Pinny would come in with a cup of cocoa on a tray, and tell me one of the stories from the quilt. She would point at a piece of the patchwork and say: "That's an interesting one," or "I remember that one well," and then she would begin. . . .

★ ★ ★

"Look at that," she said one night. "That's where the quilt began." She pointed to the very heart of the patchwork, to seven shapes stitched together in a flower-pattern, like this:

"If you look closely, you will see large, childish stitches still in the material. I've never taken them out, though I have sewn over them finely to keep them in place after all these years."

"It's like a little garden," I said. "Every shape has a different kind of flower on it, although it's hard to see what some of them are supposed to be."

"It is a garden. The flowers have faded. Real flowers always do."

"Were these real flowers?" I asked. "Honestly?"

"They were the real-est flowers in the whole world to me, when I was little."

"How little?"

"About five or six, it's hard to remember exactly. What I do remember is that we were poor in those days."

"Is it exciting to be poor?" I asked.

"There's nothing exciting or romantic about it, my child, and don't let anyone tell you otherwise. And we, of course, did not even have the luxury of admitting we were poor. We had a position to keep up. My mother was used to certain things, to certain standards in her life as far as dress and behaviour were concerned, and she would have been deeply ashamed to confess that with my father's death, everything had changed. But it had. Nobody ever discovered the economies. How I hated them! How we both hated them . . . remaking curtains into presentable dresses, collecting slivers of soap in tins, being careful all the time, thinking about every penny, and devising ways to make it stretch and do the work of tuppence. No, it was a very tiring time. When you're poor, being poor is all you have energy to think about. And, I was afraid of the dark. Mama would put me to bed by candlelight, to save gas, but she always took the candle downstairs in the end, and I lay and thought about the miles of darkness between myself and her, and covered my face with the bedclothes, every night.

"Being poor does not stop you dreaming, however, and children have a great deal of space in their heads, waiting to be filled with

dreams. I dreamed of pet animals I should have one day, of party
dresses with sashes, of coal fires in every room, of Mama riding with
me in a horse-drawn carriage, of chocolate cakes on the kitchen
table, of dolls with painted china faces—I dreamed of all sorts of
things. But what I wanted most of all, more than anything, was a
garden.

"In those days, the small, square lawn at the back of the house
was neglected. There were large, muddy patches of earth showing
through the thin blades of grass, moss spread everywhere, and it was
completely empty. Nothing grew in it, not even weeds. The shrubs
and flowers and green baize lawns of my dreams were certainly not
to be found there. I knew what a garden should be like. I'd seen them
in the Park, which we sometimes visited for a treat on Sunday. I
was quite determined to have one. I began to nag:

" 'Mama, please may I have a garden? I want a garden. Why
can't I have one?' till my poor Mama was frantic. She explained to
me gently that you had to make a garden. It was not something
you bought.

" 'I've seen flowers in the shop,' I said. 'We could buy some and
put them into the earth.'

" 'Those are cut flowers, dearest. They would fade and die at
once if you did that.'

" 'Then how do you make a garden?'

" 'The flowers grow from seeds or bulbs that you put into the
ground. If you put bulbs in now, you will have flowers when
spring comes.'

" 'Is it a lot of money for the bulbs?' I begged.

" 'We'll find it somehow,' said Mama, 'and you shall plant them
yourself.'

"I do not remember that we had trouble finding the money. I

14

was too excited at the prospect of my own garden. But now I can see that my mother must have gone without something she needed or wanted, in order to save what was necessary. One day she said: 'Come, Pinny, we'll go to the shop and buy your bulbs. I'm afraid you can only have six, though.' It sounded like a great many flowers to me.

"We spent a long time in the shop. I ran from one coloured picture to another. I looked at boxes of purple, onion-like things and wondered how they turned into daffodils and snowdrops like the ones in the park. In the end, I chose two daffodil bulbs, two hyacinths (one blue and one pink) and two red tulips. I carried the bag all the way home in my hand, and slept with it near my pillow that night.

"The next day, we took Mama's wooden spoon, and I dug holes in the wilderness at the back, while Mama watched. I put each bulb into its hole, covered it gently, and sat back to wait for the flowers to grow.

" 'Come in now, Pinny,' said Mama. 'It's getting cold.'

" 'I'm just waiting for the flowers to come,' I told her.

" 'Oh, Pinny, my love, it'll be months yet! They won't come up until the spring. Don't you understand?'

" 'When is the spring?'

" 'A long time away, really. I promise you they'll grow in the spring. When it gets warmer.'

"Time is a strange thing. It passes more quickly as you become older. Why, to me, the last five years seem no longer than a week, but when I was five and waiting for the spring, every week seemed like a year. Every week I asked: 'Is it spring yet?' and my mother would say: 'No, Pinny, you still have a long time to wait.'

"Then I caught influenza, and spent two weeks in my hot, narrow bed, dreaming of flowers and monsters, not knowing where I was.

15

At one time, my mother told me much later, they feared for my life. But I lived. I grew stronger every day, and also more and more bored, and impatient for my garden. As soon as I was allowed out of bed, I ran to the window. The garden was still mottled brown and green, and there were no flowers. I lay on my bed and wept and wept, as if I would never stop.

" 'Pinny, darling, what is it? Whatever's the matter?' said Mama. 'Why are you crying, my pet? Why?'

" 'I want my garden. You said it would grow, and it hasn't. I've waited ages and the bulbs haven't turned into flowers. I don't expect they ever will. You're horrible to tell me they will when they won't. I won't ever believe you again.'

"I can remember my mother's white face as she stood with her thin hand on the door. I knew that it was not her fault, but I needed to hurt someone, to blame someone for my disappointment. I felt wicked, and cried even louder, burying my head in the pillow. When I looked up, Mama was gone. I thought to myself:

" 'I've hurt her, and she's run away. Probably she'll never come back. I'm so naughty the flowers won't grow and I shall have no Mama.'

"This thought was so dreadful that I couldn't even cry. I sat frozen in the bed for a long time. Then Mama came in, smiling. In her hand was a small, cotton shoe-bag. She sat down on my bed.

" 'I'm going to teach you how to sew, Pinny. And the first thing we shall make will be a garden.'

" 'Can you sew a garden?' I asked.

" 'We shall do our best,' said Mama.

"First, she showed me how to hold the needle, and pull the cotton through the cloth. Then I practised stitches of all kinds, while Mama spread bits of material on my bed for me to choose from. There were flowers and leaves on every piece. My whole bed looked like a garden.

" 'This one, please. And this. And this and these two, and this one,' I said, after looking for a long time.

" 'That's enough,' said Mama. 'I have a special piece to put in the middle. Your garden should have a lawn.'

"She cut a six-sided shape out of each piece. These she put together on the table, near my bed, to show me the pattern. She took a scrap of green felt, embroidered with a tiny daisy, out of the shoe-bag and placed it in the middle. 'We'll sew these pieces together, and that'll be a little winter garden for you until your real flowers come out. And they *will* come out, you know, Pinny.'

" 'Yes, Mama, I know they will. I'm sorry.'

"I spent a long time sewing my garden together. Mama helped me, of course. It's difficult to reach into the corners. But I enjoyed it more than anything I had ever done before. Round the green felt lawn I arranged my chintz and cotton flowerbeds: roses, apple-blossom, hollyhocks, lilies, pansies, and carnations. When I finished it, it looked beautiful. I could almost smell the flowers, and I stroked my finger over the green felt, feeling the embroidered daisy in the summer grass. I had a garden. I had made it myself. It lived on the table near my bed, where I could see it every morning when I woke up, and every night when I went to bed. In my dreams, it grew and spread, the stitches turned to flagstones, and I walked on them between the flower-beds, sniffing a rose here, picking a pansy there.

"When the spring came, my real flowers bloomed at last. I was very proud of them, and of myself for planting them, and of Mama, for knowing they would grow. But they were never as sweet-smelling, nor as pretty, nor as real to me, as my own little patchwork garden."

Miss Portal
and
Miss Scripe

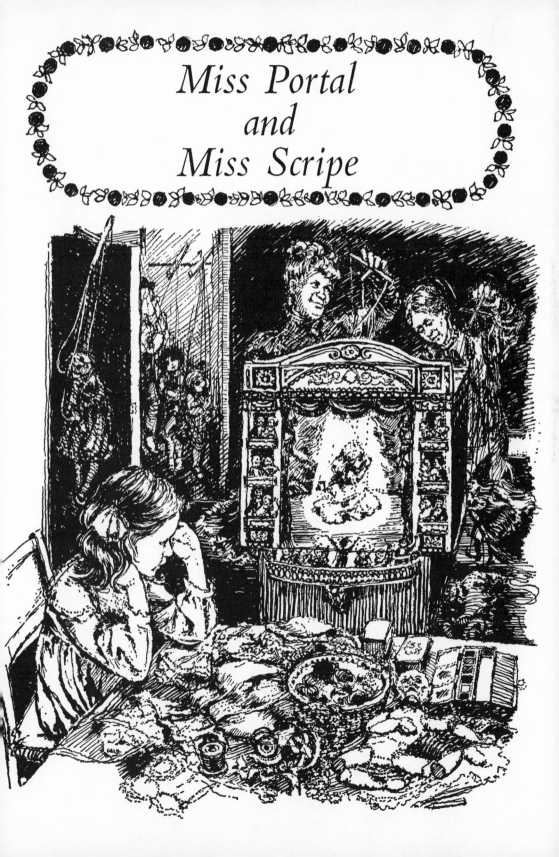

"YOU WOULD NEVER believe, would you, that this was gold satin?" said Aunt Pinny one night, pointing to a mustard-coloured patch near the foot of the bed.

"I expect it's old and it's lost its shine," I answered. "Is it from a ball gown?"

"No, no," said Aunt Pinny. "It comes from the skirt of a puppet I once helped to make. But it's a long story."

"Please tell me," I said, and lay down to listen.

"Do you remember the first few weeks at your first school? I shall never forget mine. I can remember standing in a grey, gravel yard surrounded by red brick walls with iron spikes on top. I can see the line of girls, endless, endless girls, all strangers, all taller than me, and all staring at me. I remember waving and smiling at my mother, trying to seem brave and grown-up. I can still see her wide smile and fluttering hand as she stood outside the railings and watched me walking into school for the first time.

"We all hung our shoe-bags and coats in the cloakroom on little hooks. Each hook had a label with a name written on it pasted above it. Two of the older girls helped the new girls find the right hooks, because we had not yet learned to read. The cloakroom smelled of disinfectant, cheap soap, and generations of wet coats.

"Most of all from those days, I remember the teachers, especially

21

Miss Portal and Miss Scripe. These two ladies were in charge of Form One. I first saw them standing together behind the teachers' desk in the classroom. Miss Portal was large, her nose was full of unexpected bumps, and she had a square mouth and chin. She wore her hair in an arrangement of grey sausage curls balanced on her head. These curls bounced up and down when she walked, and never lost their plumpness or came undone. Every morning they were exactly the same. Miss Portal, we decided later, must have to wake up very early to construct, each day, the same elaborate puffs and rolls.

"Miss Scripe was thin and small and wore porridge-coloured cardigans. She had straggling hair of no particular colour. Every few minutes, she stuck hair pins back into a little bun at the nape of her neck. Sometimes, the pins fell on to the floor, and we collected them for her as she walked round the classroom.

"On the first day, it was Miss Scripe who stepped forward to greet us, and said in a surprisingly firm voice: 'Good morning, gels. I am Miss Scripe, and this is Miss Portal. When you have mastered the Alphabet, I shall write our names on the blackboard. There are a few rules which you must learn if you are to be happy here. If you wish to speak, raise your hand. We have no Shouting Out in this class. You will stand when a teacher comes into the class-room, and you will bring a Clean Pocket Handkerchief every day. Is there anyone who has not brought a handkerchief to school today? Raise your hands, please.' Three girls, blushing, put up their hands.

" 'Ah, Miss Portal, I see we have three silly girls here, who do not realize the Importance of Hygiene. Shall we tell the class what happens to unhygienic children?' Miss Portal nodded, and the curls jostled one another on her head. She came and stood next to Miss Scripe and said:

" 'We provide squares of cotton for these unhappy children and they spend their Playtime hemming themselves a handkerchief. I hope none of you will forget tomorrow. I shall inspect handkerchiefs before we begin lessons.'

"I never forgot my hankie, but once or twice it fell out of my pocket on the way to school or in the cloakroom and became rather dirty, and I had to spend Playtime sitting between Miss Portal and Miss Scripe, furious at not being outside, jabbing my needle into the cotton square on my lap.

"Miss Portal taught us Sums, Nature Study, Needlework, and the Bible. Miss Scripe taught us Reading, Writing, Countries of the World and People of Long Ago. If you sat at the back of the room on a sunny day and looked at the maps and charts pinned to the walls, all you could see was a thick white layer of chalk dust, lying on the pink countries, and the green countries and blue oceans, and on the Life of a Beaver in Ten Pictures. We had a Books Monitress, a Blackboard Monitress, and a Flowers Monitress. On Monday morning, our desks were inspected. 'Tidy Desks Show Tidy Minds' Miss Scripe used to say. On Friday afternoon, our exercise books were looked at most carefully. The neat writers were given a gold star which they could stick into the back of the book. The ink-blotters and girls given to crossing out were awarded a black circle which they had to stick on the front cover of the book, for everyone to see. It was a piece of unfairness that I could never understand. Every Friday I waited in my desk, praying for a gold star, but in all my time in that class, it only happened to me twice. The fact that I never had a black circle meant nothing to me. I still remember the two pieces of work Miss Portal and Miss Scripe thought so fine. One was a map of Australia with lines of very blue wax crayon sticking out all round it, and a few kangaroos drawn at the corners

23

of the page and tidily coloured-in in brown. The other was *Tom, Tom, the piper's son* in Best Writing with not one blot.

"Naughty girls, girls who shouted out, or who had not finished their sums in the time allowed, girls who whispered together behind their books, or wrote notes to one another—they were punished by standing in front of the class with a notice hung round their neck. Miss Portal and Miss Scripe kept six such placards in their desk. There was 'Chatterbox', 'Idler', 'Cheat', 'General Nuisance', 'Naughty Girl' and my own favourite, 'Inattentive Minx'. I liked it partly because of the way it sounded, and partly because I wore it so often that I felt it was mine.

" 'Penelope, dear, come here. You are Not With Us again,' Miss Scripe would say. 'Go to the desk, and find your notice, and hang it round your neck. The classroom is not a place for dreaming, and you will learn that sooner or later. The classroom is for Study and Concentration.'

"She was wrong, of course. Classrooms are perfect places for dreaming. I could lose myself for hours, just staring at the markings and carvings on a desk, running a sharp pencil along the soft grooves in the wood, hardly aware of the rest of the class, or of the teachers until they spoke to me sharply.

"At Playtime, we skipped and ran around, and played Hopscotch and Oranges and Lemons. On cold days, we sat in the cloakroom and hid behind coats and ate our apples, and bread and butter. I cannot pretend that I was the most popular girl in my class. I was small and quiet, and although I do not think anyone really disliked me, I was nobody's special friend: the kind of child who plays on the edge of groups, always one of the last to be chosen to join in team games in the playground.

"I enjoyed my lessons for the most part. I liked dividing imaginary

buns among imaginary children. Seeing curly letters lining up on the page, one after the other, was exciting. I was even quite interested in the cat who sat on the mat and ate the rat in our reading book, and I was good at drawing pictures of autumn leaves for Nature Study. On fine days we walked in a crocodile to the park nearby to learn the names of trees. Needlework was the most disappointing subject. I had just started my patchwork quilt, and I think I felt that tacking and hemming and learning to embroider in cross-stitch was dull in comparison. Miss Portal would walk around in between the desks and look at our handiwork as we did it. 'Learn, dear gels, to sew a fine seam, and no doubt you too, like the lady in the nursery rhyme, will have strawberries, sugar and cream. That is excellent work, Belinda. You will go on to Buttonholes next week. That hem is a disgrace, Stella. Unpick it at once and begin again. I will have every stitch almost invisible, do you understand, or I will have failed in my duty. Penelope,' (to me) 'you are making progress. That cross-stitch sampler is coming along nicely. Is the back as neat as the front? I will not tolerate Messy Backs, as you know.' I turned my work over and Miss Portal wrinkled her bumpy nose, and bent her curls over my sampler. She said, 'I can just see a knot here. And here an end not properly snipped. But progress is being made. Perhaps I shall make an embroiderer of you yet.' I went on making lines of crosses in red silk, and more lines in blue silk.

"Miss Scripe was clever at drawing maps on the blackboard.

" 'This,' she would say, as she stood with her back to us and her chalk held high, 'is Africa.' And in less than a minute, there it was, every bay and inlet in just the same place as it was on the wall map. We had to take turns to come up to the blackboard and mark the main features of the landscape in with crosses. 'Penelope,' she said to me once, 'come and show the class where the Sahara

25

Desert is.' I hesitated, my chalk pointed at the middle of the continent.

" 'No, dear, still quite cool,' said Miss Scripe. I moved the chalk down a little. 'No, no, getting cooler now.' Up went the chalk. 'Yes, yes, now you're warmer, warmer, hot, hot, VERY HOT!' I made a cross and Miss Scripe said: 'Well done!' Then she sent me back to my desk, and began to draw tiny camels, and date palms and pyramids. Another girl found Central Africa and the Jungles, and Miss Scripe was happily engaged for ten minutes, drawing in gorillas, and snakes and jungle creepers. For South Africa she drew lions and bars of gold, and grapes, and diamonds. When the map was finished, she turned to face us and wiped her hands on her cardigan, leaving chalky rainbow marks.

" 'Now, gels, you must copy this map into your books, and I shall read to you while you do so.' She read to us from a large book which never mentioned that there were any people living in the countries we were colouring in. I think I was much older before I learned that Abroad was something more than rivers, mountains, animals and strange trees.

"The best part of every day was going home. When the last bell sounded, we all filed slowly and demurely out of the classroom. Once we were in the corridor, however, we ran to the cloakroom and bundled on our hats and coats and rushed to the gates. The bigger girls walked home in small groups, but mothers still waited at the railings for us. Every day, without fail, I would see my mother standing right at the front of the crowd, and I used to run all the way across the playground to greet her.

"Then, one afternoon in February, my mother was not there. My eyes filled with tears, and I could hear the beating of my own heart. But I knew that mothers were sometimes a little late. She'll be just coming down the street now, I thought to myself. She'll be here in a moment. I won't be a crybaby. She'll be here soon. I went and stood in the corner where the iron railings joined the brick wall. I could see right down the road. There was no sign of her. I stared and stared at the pavement, and willed her to come. I shut my eyes. If I count slowly to ten, and then open them, she'll be there, I said to myself. I counted, and opened my eyes, and she was nowhere to be seen. After a while, the other girls and mothers had gone, and the rain started to fall from a colourless sky on to the bare branches of the lime trees in the grey, empty streets. I started to cry then, holding on to the railings with wet hands. Suddenly, I heard a hurrying step behind me. I turned to see if by some miracle my mother had come from inside the school, although I knew that was not really possible. It was Miss Portal.

" 'What are you doing here, Penelope dear?' she said. 'Where's your mama? You must come indoors with me. It's very wet out here.' I let her lead me into school again. I was crying so much I could hardly see where I was going.

" 'Now, now, dear. Be a brave girl. Has your mama not come yet? Never mind. She has no doubt been detained by something important and will be coming presently. We often have mothers arriving a few moments late. It's very common. You come along and help me and Miss Scripe to put the classroom in order, and your mama will soon be here.'

"In the classroom, Miss Scripe was waiting. Together they dried my eyes, and took off my coat, and put me next to the bookcase to tidy it up.

" 'Big books on the bottom shelf, dear,' said Miss Scripe, 'smaller ones here.'

"This task kept me from crying for a little while. Then Miss

Portal said: 'Tell me, Penelope, do you know whether your mother ever goes out in the afternoon?'

" 'Yes, sometimes,' I answered. 'Sometimes she has to go right across London to deliver a dress. She's a dressmaker.'

" 'There you are, then,' said Miss Scripe, more to Miss Portal than to me. 'That's the answer. Mrs Pintle has maybe had difficulty in finding transport across the city. We will leave a note with the caretaker for your mama, Penelope, telling her where you are, and you shall come to tea with us. It will be a Treat.'

"Miss Scripe smiled and Miss Portal shook her curls. I put my coat on while they were writing the note, and tried to remember whether my mother had said anything that morning about delivering a dress. Perhaps she had. Tea with Miss Portal and Miss Scripe did not sound like a Treat to me, but it was kind of them, and I was glad not to be on my own without my mother. I felt a little comforted, because they were obviously not worried at all.

"It was still raining as we walked out of the gates. There were shiny grey puddles all over the pavement. Miss Portal and Miss Scripe wore galoshes and I was very surprised to see Miss Scripe jumping into the little pools, just for fun. We walked for quite a long time. In the end, we arrived at a house that looked so much like my own that I started to cry again.

" 'Now, now, dear,' said Miss Scripe. 'Don't start crying again. Your mother will be here very soon now, see if she won't. Meanwhile we shall have fun.' She opened the door, and Miss Portal and I followed her into the hall.

" 'Look all around, dear,' said Miss Portal, as she helped me take off my coat, 'and we'll prepare tea in the kitchen, which is just here. I shall call you when it's ready.'

"The house was as good as a museum. I walked all round the

front room, looking at stuffed birds, arrangements of wax fruit, dried grasses and shells under transparent domes, and heavy paper-weights with flowers swirling in blue spirals into the heart of the glass. There were photographs in padded velvet frames of men and ladies in old-fashioned clothes. There was a brass tray balanced on wooden table legs like barley sugar sticks. In a glass-fronted cabinet I found little porcelain statues of shepherds and shepherdesses in bright clothes and pointed golden slippers. Bookshelves stretched right up to the ceiling. When I had finished looking at everything I sat down on an old, green plush sofa with lumpy cushions. I did not dare to go into another room, so I just sat, feeling miserable when I thought of my mother. What had happened to her? Miss Portal and Miss Scripe had almost persuaded me that she had been delayed on a bus journey, but in my deepest self I felt the beginnings of black thoughts. Maybe she had forgotten me. Maybe she would never come back. Maybe she was dead. I started crying again.

" 'Tush, child,' said Miss Portal, who came into the room just then. 'What can I say to make you cheer up? Come and have some tea. That always helps, I find. A full stomach is the first step on the Road to Happiness.' She led me to the kitchen.

"I suppose I must have been hungry. The clock on the dresser said half past five. (Where was she? I thought.) Miss Portal gave me sweet tea in a huge cup. 'Drink it all up, and you'll find a surprise at the bottom,' she said. When I finished the tea, I looked inside the cup and saw a green fish swimming through wiggly gold lines of waves.

" 'It's lovely,' I said. 'Are there fishes in your cups, too?'

" 'Oh, yes,' they said, and I looked at their cups, but my fish was the prettiest.

" 'Have some more bread and honey,' said Miss Scripe.

" 'Have some Battenburg sponge,' said Miss Portal. This turned out to be a cake made out of pink and yellow squares.

" 'What a funny name. How do they make the pink and yellow squares stay in one place, and not get all mixed up together?'

"Miss Scripe confessed that she did not know, and many torn cookery books were consulted. They tried to explain it to me, but I had lost interest. They showed me a tea cosy knitted by Miss Portal's grandmother, and a tea-towel embroidered by last year's Infant's class.

" 'It's very pretty,' I said.

" 'Did you go into the Back Parlour?' Miss Scripe asked me, as they washed up the tea dishes.

" 'No, I was admiring all the things in the other room.'

"Miss Portal smiled, and said: 'Then the real treat is in store for you.'

" 'What is in the Back Parlour?' I said.

" 'Our secret, isn't it, Miss Scripe?' said Miss Portal.

" 'Our secret, and our hobby and our passion, and you'll love it, I'm quite sure. Let me just finish putting a shine on these cups, and then we'll go.'

"Miss Portal led the way into the Back Parlour.

" 'I'll just light the lamp, Enid,' she said to Miss Scripe, 'so hide Penelope's eyes, and I'll tell you when to look.' I stood in the dark, and Miss Scripe put her hands over my eyes.

" 'It's ready,' said Miss Portal, and Miss Scripe took her hands away. I blinked in the yellow glare, and looked all around. What I saw was nothing very extraordinary. I think I was expecting Aladdin's cave. This was very much like my mother's workroom. There was a table heaped with different scraps of fabric, a treadle sewing-machine in the corner, balls of string and heaps of sticks on another table, together with a pot of glue and some brushes. Then I saw something glorious. Against the wall stood a model theatre, almost as tall as I was.

" 'How beautiful,' I said, kneeling on the floor to look in at the stage. There were little boxes painted on each side of the stage, full of lovely ladies behind feather fans, and gentlemen with moustaches. Gilded cherubs tumbled across the top of the proscenium arch, and there was an orchestra pit, complete with musicians holding miniature instruments.

" 'The curtains are real velvet, aren't they? Do they work?' I asked.

" 'Oh yes,' said Miss Scripe. 'Everything works. It's a working puppet theatre.' She showed me the string which pulled the curtains. I tried it and they swished together at once. I pulled them open again, then closed them once more, just to see the scarlet velvet brushing across the stage.

" 'How do you work the puppets?' I wanted to know.

"Miss Portal said: 'We kneel behind the theatre like this, and drop them on to the stage from above. On strings, you see. Then we move the strings, and the puppets perform. We do all the voices ourselves.'

"I said: 'It's lovely. Where do you buy the puppets? Can I see them?'

" 'Buy them?' Miss Scripe laughed. 'Oh no, dear, we make them. All by ourselves. The dolls are stuffed cotton, with papier maché heads, and we make their dresses and suits and paint the faces. Come and see.' She took me over to a cupboard under the window.

" 'Open the door. That's it, dear. Don't be shy.' I opened it, and stepped back, a little afraid. I did not like the way the puppets were all dangling and floppy at the end of their strings.

" 'They look a little lifeless, don't they, hanging like that. But

31

later on, we'll take a couple out, and move them around for you. You'll enjoy it, you'll see.'

"Miss Scripe shut the cupboard door, and I was ashamed at the relief I felt. Silly, I told myself, they're only dolls. Only dolls, just like the ones on my bed at home.

" 'Come over here, Penelope,' said Miss Portal. 'I'm making a new princess, and you shall help me. You may hem her skirt.'

"I sat down at the table, and Miss Portal gave me a skirt made of gold satin. It was slippery stuff, and I knew that my stitches would show.

" 'I'm not very good at hemming, please, Miss Portal,' I said.

" 'Nonsense, child. This is not school. This is the theatre. I'm sure you will do very well. And if the stitches show, you can embroider over them in cross-stitch later.'

"It was pleasant sitting there, working together. I hemmed very slowly, and listened to Miss Portal and Miss Scripe talking. Miss Scripe was painting fearsome eyebrows on to the face of a wizard, and Miss Portal was sewing lace round the neck and wrists of a golden bodice that matched the skirt I had in my hands. In the end, I fell asleep with my head on the table.

"When I woke up, I felt cold. It took me few moments to remember where I was, and why, and then I started crying for my mother, and nothing Miss Portal or Miss Scripe could say would stop me. I sobbed and sobbed. Then I heard the sound of someone else crying, too. I looked around and caught sight of the model theatre. There, on the stage in a circle of light, sat a pretty young girl. I looked up, and I could just see Miss Portal and Miss Scripe kneeling in the shadow behind the theatre. I stopped crying for a moment to see why the little girl on the stage was so sad. I soon found out that she was weeping because she had lost a casket of jewels. As the girl searched for her treasure, she met a dragon, and a witch and a giant and the Spirits of the Four Winds, who all helped her. I forgot all about Miss Portal and Miss Scripe. Then I noticed the casket, half-hidden behind a rock, and I was just on the point of crying out to tell the pretty girl where it was, when I heard a loud knocking at the front door. Miss Portal and Miss Scripe stood up at once. The puppets dropped to the stage in tangles of string and wood.

" 'That'll be your mother, Penelope,' said Miss Scripe, and we almost ran to open the door. I thought, what if it's not Mama, after all, what shall I do? But it was, and I burst into tears again, as I ran and buried my face in her damp skirt. She hugged me, and comforted me, and thanked Miss Portal and Miss Scripe over and over again, there on the doorstep, with the rain blowing in all over us.

" 'Come into the parlour, Mrs Pintle. Take a glass of brandy. You look unwell.'

"It was not until we were sitting in the front room together, not until my mother began to tell us of her long journey from Richmond, and about the bus that had broken down and the endless walk to the school, and the age it took her to find the caretaker, and how she had lost her way to this house in the rain, that I realized the truth. The last four hours had been even more dreadful for her than for me. I had managed to put her out of my mind for minutes at a time, thanks to Miss Portal and Miss Scripe. She had had no one to help her, and no way of knowing that I was safe. She knew exactly what I would be feeling, and she suffered for me, as well as worrying for my safety on her account. It occurred to me then that I had not once, even in the worst depths of my misery, thought what it must have been like for her, knowing she would not be at the school gates, knowing she was making me more and more unhappy every minute she was not there. I looked at her and noticed how blotchy and swollen her eyes were.

" 'Mama,' I said, 'have you been crying, too?'

" 'Yes dear, I have. I've never cried so much before. It's the help - lessness I felt. Not being able to do anything. Not being able to tell you where I was and not to worry. It was terrible.' She began again to thank Miss Portal and Miss Scripe.

" 'It was a pleasure,' said Miss Scripe. 'We have had some fun. Penelope has been very brave, and has even helped us tonight. I'm very glad you are together now. You must come and take some nourishment, Mrs Pintle.' Miss Portal stood up and led the way to the kitchen.

"That was the end of the story. The next day I stayed away from school, on the advice of Miss Portal and Miss Scripe. The day after, I returned to the grey, gravel pavement, and the classroom. Miss Portal and Miss Scripe stood there as usual, and smiled pleasantly at us all as we took our places behind our desks. Nothing they did or said that day showed that they remembered anything about the evening I had spent with them. They did not mention it for the rest of the year.

"Then, quite suddenly, the summer term was over. Next autumn we would all be in Miss Godfray's class. Miss Portal and Miss Scripe solemnly wished us well, and reminded us about our handkerchiefs. When the final bell was rung, I stayed behind in my desk until the rest of the class had gone.

" 'Penelope, dear,' said Miss Scripe, 'come here. We have a little something for you. Something that you helped us to make when you spent the evening with us.' She opened her desk, and brought out a puppet princess, dressed in the little gold skirt I had stitched for a short while, and the gold bodice with the lace trimmings.

34

" 'This is for you,' said Miss Portal, 'you helped to make it yourself.'

" 'But I didn't really do anything. Just a few stitches. I can't take it, really I can't.'

" 'Nonsense, dear. It's yours. Now don't be silly. I hope you will be very happy with Miss Godfray. Come and see us sometimes.'

" 'Yes, I will. Thank you ever so much. For the princess. And for being so nice. Goodbye.'

"I turned and walked slowly out of the room, thinking how strange it would be not to see them every day. At the door I turned and waved. They waved back, and Miss Scripe smiled. Miss Portal was blowing her nose into a clean lace handkerchief. She blew it so hard that her curls wobbled.

"I kept the puppet princess with my dolls at home, but hardly ever played with her, because she reminded me so much of that desolate afternoon without my mother. Then I made new clothes for her, and cut the gold skirt up for the quilt. I'm glad I found it now. I'm glad to have remembered Miss Portal and Miss Scripe. Goodnight, dear."

I fell asleep before she left the room.

Mr Poffle

" 'IT WON'T DO, Mr Poffle, it won't do at all!' Mr, Gruntbussel sighed heavily, and passed a spotted handkerchief over his purple brow. 'It's not modern enough! Why my old grandmother had chintzes like these, back in the last century.' "

"Are you reciting from a book tonight, Aunt Pinny?" I asked. "The story sounds different."

"Be still, my child, and all will become clear. Now, where was I? Ah, yes, in Mr Poffle's office. I shall continue . . .

"Mr Poffle stroked his white, droopy moustache. He looked sadly at the drawing-board in front of him. Fat, white roses with shiny, green leaves, garlands of pink flowers trailing blue ribbons, riots of ivy and assorted blossom, looked smugly back at him from the paper. Mr Poffle, designer-in-chief for Gruntbussel's Textiles Inc. (World wide) had to admit that he had seen a design very much like this one not so long ago. This was hardly surprising, since he himself had produced one thousand such patterns over the last forty years.

" 'What we need,' Mr Gruntbussel continued, puffing hot breath into Mr Poffle's face, 'is novelty, a look to suit these times, electric, vibrant, full of life. These,' (he waved a bunch of fingers over the paper) 'are, quite frankly, old-fashioned. In fact they're awful. I'm afraid, Mr Poffle, I have no alternative . . .' Mr Poffle knew what was coming. When Mr Gruntbussel had no alternative, his employees had to expect the worst. In the rush of words that followed, Mr Poffle heard only the important one: *Redundant.* Gruntbussel's Textiles Inc. (World wide) were sacking him. He was out of work. Who would employ an ageing designer of cabbage roses and delicate ferns? In a fog of misery, and without a word to anyone, Mr Poffle left his office, collected his wages for that week, and walked out of the factory gates. He took his savings out of the bank, and made his way to his lodgings in the house of Mrs Brightly. He packed his few belongings carefully into a small, cardboard suitcase, and went down into the kitchen to pay Mrs Brightly the money he owed her.

" 'Well, now, lad,' said Mrs Brightly, 'home early, then? I'm just mashing meself a pot of tea. You'll have a cup won't you?'

" 'Don't mind if I do, Mrs B.' Mr. Poffle sat down. 'Reckon I need it. Yes.'

" 'What's up then, lad?' Mrs Brightly squeezed her barrel-shaped body between the chair and the table.

" 'Gruntbussel's given me the sack. Redundant, he called me. Said my drawings were old-fashioned.'

" 'Old-fashioned? Well!' Mrs Brightly could not find words to express her horror. Wasn't her entire house, cushions, curtains, chair-covers, everything, a positive jungle of Mr Poffle's prints? 'I've never heard such nonsense in my life,' she managed to splutter, after a sip of tea. 'Take no notice of him, no notice at all. Man doesn't know what's what, that's all.'

" 'But I've got the sack, Mrs B,' Mr Poffle explained patiently. 'No more work. No more money.'

Mrs Brightly understood this.

" 'Then how're you going to pay me for the room?' she whispered.

" 'I'm leaving.' Mr Poffle stirred the leaves at the bottom of his cup. 'Suitcase is outside. I only came in, really, to pay you what I owe for this week. And to say goodbye and thank you.'

"Mrs Brightly started crying. Fat, glittering tears sprinkled down her cheeks. From the heart of a storm of sniffs, sobs, grunts and moans, she told Mr Poffle that she wouldn't dream of taking any money for this week, that he'd paid her regularly for twenty years, and the least she could do was allow him one free week in all that time.

" 'After all, you'll be needing the money,' she said, wiping her eyes on her apron. 'Whatever will you do? Where will you go?'

" 'I shall go down to London, and seek my fortune. I shall search for new inspiration for my drawings, and if I find it, then one of the big London firms may give me work. One in the eye for Gruntbussel, that'd be.' Mr Poffle smiled at the thought.

" 'Where will you stay?' said Mrs Brightly.

" 'I don't know,' said Mr Poffle.

" 'Let me think now.' Mrs Brightly thought. Then, she leapt from her chair, nearly overturning the teapot, and waddled to the mantelpiece. She took down a Toby jug, and turned it upside-down over the table. That Toby jug was a cornucopia of rubbish: paperclips, broken china, old stamps, dwarf pencils with the lead missing, various coins, milk-bottle tops and pieces of old jewellery flowed on to the table in a stream. Last of all came a very ancient, torn postcard, with a view of Buckingham Palace on the front.

" 'Here you are, then. Here's Ellen Pintle's address in London. We went to the same Sunday School once. She was a lovely girl, and I'm sure she'll see you right. Copy this down.' Mr Poffle copied the address obediently into his notebook. And that is how he found himself on our doorstep quite early next morning.

41

" 'Good morning, miss,' he said to me when I opened the door. 'I wonder if I could have a word with your mother?'

" 'Yes, of course,' I said. He looked very old and tired and cold in the early morning wind, and his moustache looked floppy and sad. 'Please come inside, while I fetch Mama.'

" 'Ta!' he said, and came into the hall, where he stood holding a small, brown suitcase. When Mama came out to him, he said, 'Good morning, ma'am. My name is Mr Poffle. I'm from Leeds. I was lodging there with Mrs Brightly, who went to Sunday School with you once, I believe. She told me to come and see you.'

" 'Why, how lovely!' said Mama. 'Please come in and tell me how dear Emily is. As you may imagine, it's many years since I've seen her. It's always good to hear news of old friends.'

"We went into the parlour and drank coffee. Mama and Mr Poffle gossiped about Mrs Brightly. I was puzzled. Why was Mr Poffle so sad? What was the suitcase for? Why had he left Leeds? I said, 'Are you in London on holiday?'

" 'Oh, no,' said Mr Poffle. Then, he told us his story, as I've told it to you.

" 'You've nowhere to go, then,' I said, when he had finished.

" 'Not yet. As a matter of fact, Mrs Brightly said I was to ask you for help.' He turned to Mama. 'Perhaps you know someone who takes in lodgers?' He stroked his moustache nervously. I looked at Mama. She was hesitating, I could see. So I made up her mind for her.

" 'Mama,' I said, 'couldn't Mr Poffle stay in the spare bedroom?'

" 'Why, yes,' said Mama. 'I suppose he could.'

"Mr Poffle coughed.

" 'Madam,' he said, 'I feel that I must tell you that I am, for the moment, a little short of money. But if you will bear with me, I feel sure I will soon find employment, and I shall repay you amply for your kindness.'

" 'Why, I'm sure you will, Mr Poffle.' My mother was a little embarrassed. " 'I'm sure we shall manage splendidly until you find a suitable position.'

" 'I'm not a great eater, either, Mrs Pintle,' said Mr Poffle. 'A bird, that's what Mrs Brightly used to compare me with, when it came to the matter of eating.'

"It was all arranged. Mr Poffle unpacked his suitcase into the little chest-of-drawers and seemed very pleased with his new room. After that day, we hardly saw him. He shared breakfast and supper with us, and that was all. I began to wonder what he did all day. We knew he had no work to go to. Mama was too well-bred to ask questions, but I certainly was not. So one evening after supper, I knocked on his door.

" 'Come in,' said a muffled voice.

" 'Good evening, Mr Poffle,' I said. He was kneeling on the floor, surrounded by sheets of white paper. Paints and pencils were neatly lined up on the floor beside him. His sleeves were rolled up, and his white hair stood out from his head in feathery wisps. 'I'm disturbing you in your work. I'll go away and come another time.'

" 'Nay, lass,' he said, 'you'll stop here. I'll be glad of the company. And I'd like to know what you think of these.' He waved a hand towards the sheets of paper. 'Tell me honestly, now. What do you think? How would you like these patterns hanging as curtains in your room? I value your opinion.'

"I was thrilled. I don't think anyone had ever valued my opinion before. Certainly they had never told me they did. I looked. Now I knew what Mr Poffle did all day. He was soaking up London, looking for inspiration in the sights of the city. Hundreds of Big Bens chased each other across one page, pigeons flew past Lord Nelson a thousand times over on another, the dome of St Paul's was repeated on a third, and rows of the Peter Pan statue in Kensington Gardens covered a fourth. I didn't know what to say. I thought they were hideous. 'They're most interesting. I mean, they look very life-like. Just like the real thing. You're very clever, Mr Poffle.'

" 'You don't like them, do you?' I was silent.

" 'Well *do* you?' he insisted.

" 'No, not very much,' I admitted in the end.

" 'No more do I. Well, there it is. I tramp the streets all day, and it gladdens the heart to see how fine and handsome everything looks. But it won't do for fabrics, will it now? Couldn't abide to have Big Ben staring at me from the curtains.'

" 'They're very colourful,' I said, 'I'm sure some people would like them.'

" 'Not the kind of people I want to please,' sighed Mr Poffle. 'Ah, well, tomorrow's another day, eh? That's the thing. You never know what might be waiting for you, just around the next corner. You never know. It could be just the thing you'd been looking for for months.'

" 'It's Saturday tomorrow,' I said. 'May I come with you if Mama allows?'

" 'I'd be delighted, lass. Glad of a bit of company. Maybe you'll do the trick. Be my Muse, like. We'll go to Kew Gardens, if it's fine.'

"The next day, we set off early for Kew. Mama had made us a picnic. Mr Poffle carried his sketch pad in a string bag. He had a row of pencils in the top pocket of his jacket. My sketch book was lying on top of the food in the picnic basket. We walked around the Gardens, and after lunch, Mr Poffle took out his pencils and paper and began to copy a lilac tree. He did not say a word while he was drawing, so 1 decided to draw as well. I knew I could never copy anything I could see, so I made up something out of my head. A tree. I thought it looked quite pretty. The branches were like flames in a fire, moving about, so I coloured them orange with a wax crayon. They seemed a little empty, so I started filling them with fantastic green and black birds, creatures from dreams, insects with enormous eyes, and red, hungry-looking flowers that were bigger than the birds. I covered the whole page with my jungle, and I was just wondering what to do when I turned over, when I heard Mr. Poffle speak.

" 'Let's have a look, then, Pinny lass,' he said. I was shy about showing him my nonsense, but I couldn't refuse. He stared at it for a long time. Then, he shut his eyes and I began to feel cross. It wasn't that bad. He could at least look at it, I thought. Then he opened his eyes and looked at me, and smiled. 'I was right. You were an inspiration to me. Do you mind if I use this sketch of yours? Not copy it exactly, but adapt it a little? I've had a really grand idea. I hope you say "yes".'

" 'Do you like it?'

" 'I think it's beautiful,' he said.

" 'Then I'd be glad for you to have it.'

" 'Thank you, Pinny. I'll not forget this, and I'll let you see it as soon as it's finished.' He put my picture into his sketch book.

"For the next three days, we hardly even saw Mr Poffle at meals. I was curious about the new design. Was it going badly for him? Was that why it was taking so long? I began to worry. I worried for a whole week. Then, one day, Mr Poffle danced into breakfast. He said, 'Good morning' to us, and then turned to me: 'Pinny, the design is finished, and I should like you to be the first to see it. And then you, Mrs Pintle. Furthermore, I have here a letter. An interview has been arranged for me with Mr Mustwhistle, of Mustwhistle's Majestic Fabrics (Universal), the most important textile firm in the country. I wrote to them about this design of ours, and they are very eager to see it.' He beamed at us, and attacked his boiled eggs happily.

"After breakfast, Mama and I went up to Mr Poffle's room. The largest sheet of paper I have ever seen covered almost the whole carpet. The paper was black, and on it was my jungle, just as I had seen it in my head, very different from what I had put down on paper. There were the trees, full of fire and wind, there the birds, with feathers singing colour, and the flowers and leaves, patterned with spots and spirals. The black paper shone orange, and red and green. It took my breath away. 'It's simply wonderful,' I whispered. 'It's beautiful.'

" 'How lovely! How splendid it is!' said Mama. Mr. Poffle said,

" 'Yes, I'm quite pleased with it. I hope Mr. Mustwhistle likes it.'

" 'If he doesn't, he's stupid,' I said, and then Mama offered to sponge and iron Mr Poffle's threadbare best suit for the interview.

"I held my fingers crossed all that afternoon. It worked. Mr Poffle came home at six o'clock, with a bottle of sherry, and presents for me and Mama. She had a lacy Spanish shawl, and I had a wooden paintbox with thirty-six different colours in it. I didn't know there were so many colours in the world. Mr Mustwhistle had engaged Mr Poffle to work in the design department, and the jungle print was even now being prepared for production. We would be able to buy it in all the shops before Christmas.

" 'The name of the pattern,' said Mr Poffle,' is "Pinny". After you, my dear, because it was all your idea. Every pattern has a name, to make it easy for people to order. Mr. Mustwhistle thought it was a ridiculous name, but I said to him: "That design's called 'Pinny", and if you don't like it, I shall take it somewhere else'. He agreed at once, of course. He didn't want to lose me.' Mr Poffle laughed with pleasure.

"We bought a few yards of the jungle cloth, as soon as it was in the shops. Mr Poffle had moved out. He now lived in a little house by the river, where we used often to visit him. His moustache was trimmed and waxed, and now turned up at the ends. Mama redecorated the spare room with the 'Pinny' material, and I kept four different pieces to sew into the quilt."

Aunt Pinny pointed them out to me: a leaf, a bird, a flower, and a branch that flickered like a flame.

Rose

AUNT PINNY LOOKED out of the window. She said:

"The square was different, many years ago. Little girls used to walk along the paths in frothy dresses with blue sashes, boys played marbles and bowled hoops as they ran past. Padded nannies, with metal clasps on their belts, wheeled their starched and ribboned babies in high perambulators. I longed to talk to some of the girls and boys, but they never stopped to talk. Perhaps their mothers had said they were not to speak to a child dressed in such an unladylike mixture of fabrics. My mother often sent me out to play in a dress made from cut-out chair covers, or her last year's 'good black'. I even had a pinafore made from an ancient evening gown, and this, I thought, was quite a grand outfit until I went into the square.

"In November of that year, the streets were often deserted because of the fogs that settled over London in the early evenings. Not like the flimsy little mists you get now, these were called 'pea-soupers', and they were as thick as the thickest soup you ever saw. I loved the fog, and sometimes, on afternoons when my mother had to deliver a dress in another part of town, I used to slip out of the house, and wander around the square, trying to catch handfuls of it: yellow near the lamp posts, and green-brown in the spaces in between. It was easy to pretend you were under the sea, or the only person left on earth. Imagine my surprise, then, when I saw a tall, cloaked figure standing hardly a foot away from me. I was not afraid, for the folds of the cloak were gentle, and the voice that came from beneath the wide hood was soft and soothing:

" 'My child, I fear I have frightened you,' said the lady. 'I'm sorry, it's very silly of me, but I have lost my way in the fog. Do you not think that is strange? In this square, outside my very own house? Do you live in the square, too? Why are you out alone on such an afternoon?'

" 'Yes, ma'am, I live at number 11, and I'm out because I like the fog. You can hide in it, and everything is rubbed out and soft around the edges.'

" 'Well, I'm sure you must be frozen to death, poor child. Come and help me find Number 27, and I shall make you a warm drink when we are inside.'

"I could not remember having seen Number 27 in the square, but I was very young, and the square was very big, and I was sure the lady knew more than I did about such matters. Besides, I did want a warm drink. So we slid around the square, going right up to every door to look at the numbers. It seemed to me we walked for miles and hours, and out of the London I knew into a dim, silent land where the fog pressed down on your eyes, like a velvet mask. At last, however, we found it: Number 27.

"I can feel the warmth of that house as I speak of it now. All the light in the world seemed to have taken refuge in those high rooms, hiding from the fog. I could see the lady properly now. All I can say about her is this: she was both young and old. Her face was unlined, but her hair was white. She trod lightly on the thick carpets, but she wore the black, high-necked dress of a grandmother. We went into a red room, where a log fire crackled and smoked, and I

52

sat in an armchair. while she went to prepare the drink. I think I fell asleep for a moment or two. I was awakened by the rattle of crockery. The lady was sitting near a small table, pouring coffee from a silver pot.

" 'Not really a child's drink,' she smiled at me, 'but as a special treat, just this once. There' (she handed me the cup). 'Now tell me how your dear mama is. I know her well. I knew you when you were tiny. You're Penelope Pintle, aren't you? Tell me all about yourself.'

"I told her about my school, the books I was reading, and my friends. I was curious to know all about her, too, but children do not have the same right to ask as grown-up people do. I tried to think of a suitable question that would tell me what I wanted to know. 'Have you any children?' I ventured finally. I thought at first it was the wrong question, so long and deep was the silence which followed. But it was not.

" 'Yes, I have a child. Her name is Rose. She is two years old. My old Nanny looks after her for me. Poor Nanny! She's not very sprightly, and Rose can be so naughty. Yet it is difficult to scold such a child. She has a smile that would melt stones. My husband died last year, and so you see, there's only me. And Nanny.'

" 'Is Rose sleeping now?' I whispered.

" 'Yes, she's fast asleep, and Nanny with her. They look as if nothing would wake them. Would you like to creep up to the nursery and have a look?'

" 'Oh, yes, please!' I said, for I loved babies, and was never allowed to peep into the heavily guarded perambulators in the square. The lady took a lamp in her hand, and we went up and up, past many paintings of stiff ladies and gentlemen in antique clothes. The stairs never once creaked, I remember. It was a house of utmost stillness, a house asleep. In the baby's room, the yellow candlelight danced on the bridle of an old rocking horse. Rose was lying on her side, her face turned to the light. From the next-door room, I could hear Nanny snoring. I put out my hand, and touched the baby's cheek. It was the softest thing I had ever touched. I said: 'Rose is a lovely name for her. She is just like a little pink rose.' I could not think of anything else to say that would express the love I felt, and the happiness. We went downstairs in silence. In the hall, I said: 'I think I must go home now, or Mama will worry. Thank you very much for everything, and especially for letting me look at Rose.'

" 'I have to thank you,' she said, 'for helping me to find my way home. I have a small present for you, to show my gratitude. There's some pretty cotton here—just enough for your Mama to make you a dress. See, it has pink roses on it to remind you of my baby. They will never fade.'

"She had opened a chest, and taken out a roll of soft, white cloth, scattered all over with tiny roses, pink and just on the point of opening. Each bud was tightly held between green leaves. I was speechless, and blushing with pride and pleasure as I left the house in confusion, clutching the material under my arm. I ran across the square, and hammered on the door of our house. My mother opened it at once.

" 'Mama, look, it's me. Look what I've been given! Look, you can make me a *real* dress, with yards of stuff in the skirt, and frills, and isn't it lovely, all the pink roses? I could have a pink sash . . .'

" 'Calm down, Pinny, calm down,' said my mother. 'Wherever have you been? I've been so worried. What have you been doing? Take a deep breath, and tell me everything.'

"I told my mother the whole story, just as I have been telling it to you. When I had finished, I noticed how pale and quiet my mother was.

" 'Someone must have given you the material,' she muttered, half to herself. 'All the shops are closed. Are you sure it was Number 27?'

" 'Of course I'm sure. I remember thinking that I'd never noticed the number before.'

" 'No,' said my mother. 'Mrs Mackenzie, the lady from Number 27, moved away to the country many years ago. The gentleman in Number 25 bought her house, and demolished it. He had the land made into a walled garden for his house. Mrs Mackenzie never had a child, although she wanted one, very much, I know that. She doted on you, when you were a tiny baby.'

" 'Did I see . . . a ghost? Was Rose a ghost?' I whispered.

" 'I don't know what you saw, Pinny, but there never was a baby, and I do wonder where this material came from. It is very strange. Go to bed now, my love, and try to sleep, and tomorrow I shall make you a lovely dress.'

"I had my dress, and wore it about the square with great pride. I cannot remember after all this time whether people stopped to talk to me, now that I was properly dressed. What I do remember is that for a long time, months and months, I used to stand every day outside the walled garden of Number 25, and think about Rose. On summer nights, the fragrance from the garden floated right across the square, and into our house. I kept the dress for a long time, and only cut it up for the patchwork years later. All these things I've been telling you took place nearly sixty years ago, and you see Mrs Mackenzie was right. The little roses have not faded at all."

A Zebra for Helen

AUNT PINNY SAT at the foot of my bed, gently stroking a small patch of black and white striped material.

"Why are you stroking that?" I asked.

"Because it reminds me of Helen. She was my first real friend, and these stripes remind me of the day I first met her. Shall I tell you about it?"

"Yes, please," I said, and pulled the quilt up round my shoulders.

"Helen comes into the story at the end, although, as you shall see, she's very important. It all began a few weeks before Christmas. I was six years old. My mother was spending every spare moment cutting, stitching and stuffing soft toys. They were not for me. They were to be sold at the Christmas Jumble Sale in our Church Hall, to raise money for a nearby Orphanage. I longed for some of them, though. There were velvet rabbits, elephants with silken ears, and a chicken trimmed with real feathers. There was a plush cat with huge, gold buttons for eyes and a tiny felt mouth. There was even a lion with real woollen strands standing out round his head. I said to my mother:

" 'Why don't you ever make animals like these for me?'

" 'Because, child, I have our living to earn. My dresses would never be finished if I spent all my time on toys.'

" 'But you're spending all your time on toys now,' I muttered, near to tears.

"My mother put down the satin snake she was sewing. 'Darling, that's for Charity. And besides, you know Miss Snow. It's very hard to say "no" to such a lady!'

"That was true. Miss Snow, our Vicar's sister, was a solid mountain of a woman, tightly squeezed into grey dresses so stiff they seemed to be made of metal. She had hard blue eyes like marbles, and smiling was something she almost never did.

" 'If you like I'll cut you out a pattern,' my mother went on, 'and you can sew your own little animal.' She looked through the basket of materials on the sofa beside her. 'How about this? We could make a small zebra.' She held out a piece of black and white striped cotton.

" 'Can't I make a velvet rabbit instead?' I asked her.

" 'I'm afraid not, Pinny dear. Miss Snow asked for a great many rabbits. It seems they are very popular with the children, and I haven't very much velvet left. I'm sorry.'

"I could see it was no use at all. I felt angry and miserable, and determined not to take the least bit of trouble over the zebra. I nearly said I didn't want to make one at all, but I was bored and my mother was busy, so I thought I might just as well sew as do anything else. 'I'll try a zebra, then. Will you cut it out for me, please.'

"To watch my mother cut something out was a treat. Snip went the silver scissors and there was an ear, snap and there was a leg, snip, snap, snip and there were two identical zebra-shaped pieces lying on the carpet, so life-like that they almost seemed to be prancing away on their tiny hooves. I began to like the zebra a little.

" 'Now you must sew all round the edges, dear, neatly, mind

you, and leave the tummy open for the stuffing. We'll sew it up at the end.'

"I sat on a stool beside my mother and sewed as neatly as I could. I pricked my finger once, in spite of my thimble, and a little drop of blood fell on the material. I rubbed it off at once, but it left a mark. I tried to sew over the stain, but a little bit still showed. I thought: 'I don't care. It'll be a rotten old zebra, anyway.' I stitched and stitched and after a while, my zebra was ready to be stuffed. I showed it to my mother.

" 'That's lovely, dear,' she said, but she didn't mean it. It was just that she didn't want to hurt my feelings. I thought that maybe it would look better when it had been stuffed, and I said so. My mother looked relieved. 'Oh, I'm sure it will. Let's stuff it at once.'

"We pushed small pieces of rag into the gaping stomach, and sewed it up. I sewed on two black buttons for eyes, and my mother embroidered a red mouth, and then we looked at it, standing lopsided on the carpet. I burst into tears.

" 'Pinny, love, what's the matter? There's your lovely zebra that you made yourself. You should be proud. Why ever are you crying?'

" 'When you cut it out it was *really* a zebra, small and prancing and so pretty, but now I've sewn it, it's lumpy and its back is crooked, and its ears aren't the right shape and it can hardly stand, and it's got a spot of my blood on it. I don't like it, and I don't want to keep it.'

"In the end, my mother calmed me down with a cup of warm milk, and the promise of a whole sixpence to spend at the Jumble Sale, on whatever I liked. I went to bed that night and dreamed of my crooked zebra, unable to run through the grass with his real zebra friends.

"Next morning, I gave the zebra to my mother for the Soft Toy Stall, and she was very pleased. 'If you don't want it, I'm sure there's some child who will. Thank you, Pinny. I shall tell Miss Snow that it's your contribution, and I shall put it right at the front of the stall.'

"I spent the next few days thinking about how I would spend my money. On the day of the Jumble Sale, my mother wrapped the sixpence in tissue paper, and put it into my pocket. I felt it with my fingers every few minutes as we walked to the Church Hall, just to make certain it was still there, safe.

"The Church Hall looked splendid. Usually, it was a brown and green box with a dusty stage at the far end, full of little draughts of wind that puffed around your feet. But now it was decorated with holly wreaths and red ribbons and paper lanterns, and filled with stalls full of treasures. I didn't know where to look first, and I was standing in the doorway deciding where to go, when Miss Snow in a shiny, steel dress (shiny, because this was an occasion) pushed her way between the stalls towards us. She ignored me completely, but she said to my mother:

" 'Ah, capital, Mrs Pintle. All ready for the fray, I see. Good, good. The public will be arriving in half an hour. Would you be so good as to put the finishing touches to your stall? Thank you so much.' She gathered her skirts together and ploughed back to where she came from. My mother hurried away. I looked around. Ladies behind each stall were arranging, rearranging, counting out piles of pennies, smoothing their hair, smiling, fluttering fingers to their brooches, waving to one another. One other person was standing about, like me, and that was the Vicar. He was a small, mouse-like man, with soft, white hands and soft, white hair. He came and spoke to me for a while, about how lovely the Hall looked, and how hard everyone had worked, and about what I was going to buy, until Miss Snow towed him away to help sort out the second-hand books. I was left alone to look at everything.

"Some stalls I didn't even stop at. I wasn't interested in pots of home-made jam, or ugly vases, or second hand baby clothes. I didn't need lace mats, or unpolished brass candlesticks, or pin cushions. My mother's stall was the best. It would have looked like a whole zoo of wonderful animals, if it were not for my zebra right in the front row. I looked at him for a long time. It seemed to me as though the other animals were staring at him out of their button eyes, as if to say: 'Whatever are *you* doing here? You should go somewhere else. We are beautiful beasts, while you are not beautiful at all.' I was surprised to find myself feeling cross with the other soft toys. I even turned one particularly smug tiger right round, because he was looking so pleased with himself that I didn't want to see his face. I said to the zebra, in a whisper:

" 'Don't worry, I'm sure someone will want you and buy you very soon.'

"As I wandered away, I was quite surprised at what I'd done. Could I be growing fond of the zebra I'd made? It was not really fondness, I decided. I was just feeling a little sorry for it.

"People began to come into the Hall just then, and soon it became filled with voices, and the smell of coats, and the rustle of best dresses. Hats blossomed like flowers against the brown walls, rings shone in the light, children pulled at skirts, hands touched and picked up, and put down, eyes looked, purses came out of bags, and precious bargains were laid in baskets.

"I stood for a long time near the Dolls' Stall, trying to decide whether I wanted another. Dolls are strange: you either take to them or you don't. These dolls all had pouting mouths, hair that was too yellow, gowns that were too fine. I could not imagine loving a single one of them. I moved on.

"Then I saw it. It was a musical box, playing 'Goodbye, Dolly Gray'. It was the most enchanting thing I had ever seen, and I wanted it with all my heart. The wooden lid was painted in a pattern of plump, pink flowers and glossy blue ribbons, and right in the middle there was a picture of a lady dancing in a shower of tiny, black notes of music: crotchets, and quavers and semi-quavers. The lady's dress was blue, with a full skirt. As soon as I could make myself heard above the noise, I asked the lady behind the stall how much the musical box cost.

" 'What box, dear? Oh, that old thing. That's only a shilling.'

"My fingers crushed the sixpence in my pocket. Only half enough. What was I going to do? My mother would have to give me a whole new sixpence. Maybe she wouldn't want to? I pushed that thought away quickly. Surely she would want me to have the lovely box? Would someone else buy it in the time it would take me to walk to the Soft Toy Stall, and back? They were almost bound to, because it was the prettiest thing in the Hall. I decided to stay near the box all afternoon, and touch it whenever anyone came near it. Then they would think I was buying it. As soon as people began to leave the Hall at the end of the afternoon, I would rush back to my mother and ask for the money.

"The time passed quickly. I played 'Goodbye Dolly Gray' over and over again, and hardly noticed the other people. After a while, they began to leave the Hall. Outside it was dark. This, I thought, would be a safe moment to rush to my mother and ask her for another sixpence.

"She was sitting on a chair behind her stall, looking very happy. Her hair was a little untidy, and her cheeks were pink.

" 'Mother,' I said, 'I'm so sorry, but I've found just what I'd like and it costs a shilling. Please, *please* can you give me another six-pence?'

" 'Aren't you even going to tell me what it is?' My mother smiled at me.

" 'A musical box, with a dancing lady, and flowers. It plays "Goodbye Dolly Gray". It's beautiful.'

" 'Well, it sounds very nice, dear, I'm sure.' She pushed some strands of hair away from her forehead. 'As I've done so well and sold nearly all my animals, and since it's nearly Christmas, I suppose you may have an extra sixpence, just this once.'

"I ran behind the stall, and hugged my mother's knees, while she counted out the money. I looked up. My mother had put six separate pennies out on the red cloth of the stall. I noticed, briefly, that my zebra was the only animal that had not been sold, and I felt a little sad for him, but I was longing to go back to my box, and so happy at the thought of owning it, and stroking it, and hearing the twinkling music in my very own room that I forgot about the zebra as soon as I had collected the six pennies together.

"I fled back to pay for my musical box. It was gone. I looked under the cloth that covered the stall, under embroidered tray cloths, behind all the ornaments lying on the stall. It had gone. I couldn't believe it. I said to the lady:

" 'Please, where is the musical box?'

" 'Sold, dear, I'm afraid,' she answered, putting things away into brown boxes. 'Just a few moments ago. I didn't know you were interested in buying it.'

"Again, I could not believe it. Had she not even seen me there, all afternoon, stroking the lid? Had she not heard the music? I

65

stared at the lady's drooping cheeks, and her plum-coloured dress and nearly burst with pure anger. I hated her.

"I walked back to my mother's stall. I didn't know where I was. I forgot about people, and bumped into knees and baskets feeling nothing, feeling numbed. All I knew and all I could think of was the deep, black hole of disappointment and loss that had taken the place of all the pleasure I had felt when I thought I owned the box. Gradually, I began to notice what was around me. I was standing beside my mother's stall, and the zebra was looking up at me, quite kindly, I thought. My misery and the zebra's loneliness on the counter became mixed up together. It seemed that no one else wanted him, so he would be mine, after all. I paid my mother a shilling for him. I didn't need the money for anything now, and I thought it would make the zebra feel more important if he were a bought animal, and not simply a left over. I pulled him off the stall and hugged him. He was soft and comforting. Then I went and sat on the steps by the side of the stage, out of sight of my mother, and wept and wept into the zebra's black and white back.

"I don't know how long I sat there, crying, but after a while, I noticed a shiny pair of black boots on the floor, buttoned firmly around two short legs. Then came a cherry-red skirt, trimmed with white fur, a tight red jacket, with fur at the neck and wrists, and then a face. The face belonged to a girl, with round cheeks and a straight fringe of dark hair. Her eyes were brown and bright and very wide open. She was chewing her bottom lip, and clutching a white fur muff. The string dangled and dragged on the dirty floor. She said:

" 'You've been crying for ages.'

" 'Yes,' I managed to mutter.

" 'Have you finished crying now?'

66

" 'I think so, thank you. I'll cry again later.'

" 'Why are you crying, anyway? I wouldn't cry, not with a zebra like that.'

" 'Do you like it?'

" 'Yes,' said the girl, firmly. 'I like animals. I like sick animals best, because then I can play animal hospitals, which is my favourite game. Your zebra looks *very* sick. That's why I like him.'

" 'I made him,' I said.

" 'Oh, my!' (the brown eyes opened wider) 'how clever of you, to make a sick zebra.'

" 'You can have him. I don't really want him. I only took him because I felt sorry for him. Nobody bought him, you see.'

" 'I would've, if I'd seen him,' said the girl. 'Thank you, though, very much, for giving him to me. My name is Helen Arthur. What's your name?'

" 'Pinny,' I said. 'Well, Penelope Sophia Pintle, really, but that's long, so I'm called Pinny.'

" 'I haven't very much I can give you in return, I'm afraid. Only a silly little box thing my Nanny bought for me.' From her muff she took out my box, with the dancing lady on it, and almost threw it into my lap.

"I think Helen was very surprised when I jumped up and hugged her. I was quite surprised myself. I almost shouted:

" 'Oh, I love you, Helen, I love you. You're my friend! You are my friend, aren't you?'

" 'I don't really know you, but you look nice. I will be your friend if you like.'

" 'We held hands and went over to where my mother was putting her coat on.

" 'Is that your mother?' asked Helen.

67

" 'Yes, in the brown dress.'

" 'She's talking to my Nanny.'

" 'Haven't you got a mother?' I wanted to know.

" 'Yes, but she goes out a lot, so Nanny looks after me most of the time.'

"I went up to my mother, and told her about Helen giving me the musical box. Helen said to her Nanny: 'Please can Pinny come to tea tomorrow?' And, of course, Nanny said 'yes' and my mother said 'yes'."

Aunt Pinny got up.

"Is that the end of the story," I murmured.

"Yes, and the beginning of my friendship with Helen. We've been friends ever since. She's an elderly lady now, like me, I suppose. But she looks just the same to me as she did then, so many years ago. She still wears a cherry-red coat."

"But how did you come to have the patch for your quilt, if Helen had the zebra?"

Aunt Pinny laughed. "Zebra was operated on in Helen's animal hospital almost immediately. We cut a big piece out of his side and replaced it with a bit of red felt. That was the scar, you see. I kept the cut-out black and white piece and sewed it into the quilt. Goodnight, now."

Aunt Pinny switched off the light and went out of the room.

The Adventures of
Major Variana

"THAT BLACK PATCH is very dull," I said to Aunt Pinny one night.

"It looks dull, certainly," she agreed. "It is only black worsted, after all. But it is full of memories of Major Variana, who was a most unusual gentleman, and who turned out to be . . . well, shall I tell you the whole story?"

"Yes, please," I said, and settled myself down to listen.

"I've told you, haven't I, about the garden in the middle of our square? One night, just as it was beginning to grow dark, I was looking out of the window. It was spring, and I liked the way the evening turned the branches of the trees into pale mists of blossom. I could smell the lilac. Battalions of scarlet tulips stood to attention in crescent-shaped beds. Ladies and gentlemen sometimes strolled in the garden at this hour, before their evening meal, and I enjoyed looking out and admiring the pearly shirt-fronts and soft dresses, the curled hair and the satin shoes with high heels and straps across the front. On this particular evening, I was watching a young couple talking on one of the benches. Suddenly I heard an unfamiliar sound in the distance. I could tell that someone was walking towards the garden from the other side of the square, and his step frightened me. As I listened to the walk-tap-walk, walk-tap-walk coming closer, I imagined a giant striding down the path, picking blossoms from the trees as he passed by, as if they were flowers growing in the earth.

"When I saw the man coming out of the garden on our side of the square, I almost laughed, so different was he from my imagined giant. He was quite an ordinary person, really, dressed in black, and holding an ebony cane. There was nothing strange about him, except his limp. I suppose I must have been very young. The limp terrified me more than a real giant would have done. The man's whole body rose and then fell, rose and fell rhythmically, as if he were walking on the waves of an invisible sea. I turned quickly away from the window and said to my mother, who was reading beside the fire:

" 'Look, Mother. Please come and look.'

"She must have heard the fear in my voice, because she put her book down at once and came to the window. I said:

" 'Do you know who that man is? Why does he walk like that? I don't like it.'

" 'Why, silly, maybe he hurt his leg, perhaps in the Boer War. Or maybe he was born with one leg shorter than the other. He seems a well set-up, sprightly gentleman in spite of the leg, but I don't know who he is, I'm afraid. I don't remember having seen him before.'

"My mother's explanation for the limp did not really comfort me. I spent the whole evening wondering which would be worse: to have your leg so badly hurt, or to be born with one short leg. In the end, I decided it would be better not to be hurt. I hated pain of any kind, and I'm afraid I used to make the most dreadful fuss at the slightest little cut or bruise. I felt sorry for the man in the square. He must be very brave, because he wasn't crying. He must have been a soldier once, to be so brave. Or perhaps the leg had stopped hurting by now. I hoped so.

72

"The next time I saw him was a few weeks later. Again, he was walk-tap-walking round the square, upright in his black suit. That afternoon my mother was entertaining Miss Frowse to tea, and that turned out to be very fortunate. Alice Frowse was the biggest gossip in the square. She was quite possibly the biggest gossip in the whole of London, for she seemed to know as much about the affairs of the King and nobility as she knew about those of all her neighbours. My mother made dresses for her twice a year, and I thought they were splendid: sequined, ribboned, laced and trimmed with braid. My mother muttered: 'Most unsuitable for a lady of her years,' every time she made one. We looked forward to her visits, however, because, as my mother often said, she was as good as a newspaper.

"I turned away from the window, as soon as I saw him, and said to our visitor:

" 'Miss Frowse, do you know who this gentleman is? He looks very interesting.'

"The word 'interesting' was enough. Miss Frowse had been about to pop a morsel of iced sponge cake into her mouth between stories, but she put it down at once, and came to look out of the window.

" 'Why, Pinny, that's Major Variana. Surely I have told you about him before? He is, indeed, a most fascinating gentleman.'

" 'Does "Major" mean he's a soldier? Why is he not wearing a uniform?'

" 'He *was* a soldier,' Miss Frowse began, and then I saw that she was waving her hand to him through the window. He must have felt us looking at him, for he suddenly turned his face towards us, and doffed his cap most politely. My mother by this time was standing with us at the window.

" 'Do you know him, Alice?' she asked.

"'Why yes, of course, Ellen.' Miss Frowse sounded shocked. 'I'm not in the habit of waving to strangers.'

"'Then please invite him in to take tea with us. We should seem inhospitable otherwise, and to be sure, he does seem fascinating.'

"Miss Frowse did not hesitate. She opened the front door just as he was passing by, and we heard her say:

"'Major Variana, such a pleasure . . . take tea with a very good friend of mine . . . please come in.'

"I could hear the stick tapping up the stone steps, then a muffled tap and walk through the hall, and then Miss Frowse rustled in with the Major behind her. 'Ellen, my dear, this is Major Variana. Major, may I present my very good friend, Mrs Ellen Pintle' (my mother stepped forward and shook hands with the Major) 'and her little girl, Pinny.' My mother pushed me towards the man in the black suit, and I held my hand out, still feeling frightened. I tried as hard as I could, but didn't manage to stop myself staring at the Major's legs. They both looked exactly the same length.

"'Please sit down,' my mother was saying, 'and make yourself comfortable.' The Major settled himself on the sofa, and put his ebony cane on the floor beside him. I was longing to pick it up and look at it carefully, because it was carved at the top into the shape of a lion's head. I suppose I must have been staring at it, because the Major said:

"'Pinny, would you like to look more closely at my stick?' I nodded. 'Then please do.' I rushed over to the sofa and picked it up. The lion's eyes were made of mother-of-pearl, and there were small chips of ivory for his teeth.

"'It's very nice,' I said.

"'I'm glad you like it, Pinny,' said the Major. 'It was a thank-you present from an African chief after I had rescued his son from

74

the jaws of a lion. Thank you, Mrs Pintle, I should love a scone.'

"I was spellbound. He must be the bravest man in the world, rescuing children in Africa. Maybe the lion had bitten or clawed his leg? I was longing to question him, but Miss Frowse was asking him how the Grand Duke was keeping. What was a Grand Duke? I had no idea, but I knew dukes were quite important, so I supposed a Grand Duke must be even more important than a duke. I stared at Major Variana, looking for signs of grandness and bravery in his face. All I saw was an ordinary man, a little thin, with brown eyes that seemed to be laughing all the time. He had grey hair, parted in the middle, and wore a high, white collar. His hands were quite rough and brown, just the sort of hands you would expect on someone who fought with lions. Maybe he had shot the lion, though? That was more likely. Miss Frowse said:

" 'Major, I'm sure you've told your stories many times to many people, but Mrs Pintle and Pinny too, I'm sure, would be *so* thrilled to hear some of your adventures.'

"The Major coughed, and said: 'I'd be delighted, of course, but it's a little difficult to know where to begin . . .'

"I said, quickly: 'Please, sir, how did you hurt your leg?' and then I blushed, in case I was being impolite.

" 'That!' The Major laughed. 'A rather hungry crocodile in the upper reaches of the Nile fancied my toes for breakfast.'

" 'You mean, he bit them right off?' I was appalled.

" 'No, no, dear child. Don't distress yourself,' said the Major. 'One of my fellow officers shot the devil instantly. All the crocodile had time for was a fairly short chew, you understand. Nothing too serious.'

"I was silent. The Major bit into his second scone. He said:

75

" 'Shall I cheer you up? Shall I tell you about the time I had to make a tiger cough? He had tried to swallow a priceless emerald, and the stone stuck in his throat. Do you know what I did? I blew strong cigar smoke in the tiger's face, after my men and I had wrapped him in a stout net. He coughed and coughed, and out came the emerald.' I smiled at the thought of a coughing tiger.

" 'Why did you not kill him?'

" 'He was, believe it or not, a Princess's pet. Kept in the grounds of the palace at the end of a long, gold chain. The princess always said he would never hurt her, and indeed, he never did, but that didn't prevent him from gobbling up her emerald ring. She had taken it off to go bathing, and left it among her clothes, within reach of the tiger.' The Major laughed. 'We must have looked very funny, my three helpers and myself, rushing after the tiger, holding a huge net by the corners like a sheet. Not so funny when the tiger began to chase us. We nearly let go of the corners, I can tell you!'

" 'How did you catch him in the end?' I asked. The Major roared with laughter.

" 'I tripped him up. Yes, with my foot, and he fell right into the net. We bundled him up like a baby, and then I began puffing smoke in his face. The whole episode was vastly amusing.'

"I was thrilled. The Major was obviously quite fearless. Tripping up a tiger, even a tiger on the end of a long chain, was not my idea of amusement. I shivered pleasantly.

" 'Please tell some more,' I said.

" 'Well, now,' said the Major, 'what would you like to hear? About the time when I escaped from captivity by hiding in a laundry bag? About my journey from Polynesia to China in an open boat? Oh, the splendid storms, typhoons and hurricanes I could tell you about! Have you ever seen a wave as tall as a house? Palm trees uprooted as if they were radishes? Roofs flying about in the air like straw birds?'

" 'Have another cup of tea, Major,' said my mother.

" 'Thank you, Mrs Pintle, I'd love one.' The Major held out his cup and saucer. Then he turned to me:

" 'Once,' he began, 'I was riding in a horse-drawn sled across a great frozen plain in Russia. I was fleeing, in fact. Being chased by a jumped-up nobody of a princeling with a small mind and a large moustache. I had wounded him slightly in a duel, and he was after my blood, I assure you. All the food I had with me was a string of sausages, which I had luckily bought that very day. There I was, then, sliding and crunching through the frozen landscape, with the shouts of that abominable man and his companions floating behind me on the wind. I passed a small clump of pine trees on my right, and out of the trees, just to add to my troubles, came a pack of wolves. They're always called "ravening wolves," aren't they, in stories, and I could see why. Hungrier-looking beasts I have never seen. Yellow eyes, they had, and thin, mean faces. All of them were after me. What was I to do? I was somewhat at a loss, I can tell you, until I remembered the sausages. I also remembered that I was the champion thrower-in-of-balls from the deep field in regimental cricket matches. So I chucked the sausages as hard as I could, and they sailed over the horrible, grey heads, and landed on the snow behind the last wolf in the pack. He began to tear them apart, and his friends, not wishing to miss the feast, turned their backs on me, and joined in the tearing. My horses were mercifully carrying me away, but I just managed to see the wolves finish the sausages, and begin to run in the other direction. They were now chasing the princeling and his men, who had almost ridden straight into them,

77

back to where they came from, and jolly good riddance to them, I say.'

" 'It was lucky you had the sausages,' I said, 'but you must have been very hungry without them.'

" 'I was,' the Major smiled. 'Just thinking about it makes me hungry all over again, so I'll have a slice of that cake, if I may.'

"The Major told more stories, and ate more cake. He told of cavalry charges, and sieges, battles and triumphal marches, parades, captures, and escapes. My eyelids began to drop over my eyes. The Major's tales were muddled in my head, pictures filled my drowsy mind: Major Variana in a scarlet and gold uniform on a huge, black horse charging the enemy, tigers, wolves, crocodiles and emeralds. The last thing I remembered before I fell asleep was the glowing mother-of-pearl eyes of the Major's lion-headed cane, changing colour in the firelight.

"The next day, Major Variana seemed very far away. I almost felt as though I had dreamed it all. I said so to my mother.

" 'No, dear,' she said, 'it was real enough. And wasn't he an interesting man? Why, if I had had all those adventures, I should write them all down in a book.'

" 'It's hard to think of him doing all those brave things,' I said. 'He looks so ordinary.'

" 'Why, Pinny, I thought he looked most distinguished. I could well imagine him in uniform.'

" 'I can't really,' I said, and started buttering another piece of toast.

" 'Miss Frowse met him at a party, she says,' my mother murmured. 'She manages to meet everybody.' She poured herself another cup of tea, and we began to talk about something else.

"I looked out of the window every evening, hoping to see the Major, but a month passed, and he did not appear again. Perhaps,

I thought, he was away having another adventure. In time, I forgot all about him.

"Then, a few months later, when my friend Helen and I were coming home from school, I saw him walking ahead of us on the pavement. There was no mistaking the walk-tap-walk and the straight black back. I don't know why I did not call out to him. After all, we had been introduced. I said to Helen: 'That's the Major. I wonder where he's going?'

" 'Let's follow him and see,' said Helen, who was almost as daring as the Major himself.

" 'We'll be late home,' I said.

" 'Don't be silly,' said Helen. 'We won't follow him very far. Come on.'

"We walked for quite a long time. I was scared that he would catch us, scared of the darkness creeping up around us, scared of the shabby little streets we were walking through. Helen was scared of nothing, so I followed her and hoped for the best. Finally, the Major went into a shop. It was a greengrocer's, with a sign over the front that said: 'Fruit and Vegetables. Best Quality'.

" 'He's probably stopped to buy some apples,' said Helen.

" 'Let's go home now, Helen, please,' I said.

" 'Don't be such a cowardy custard,' Helen muttered. 'Come and peep into the window and see what he's doing.'

"We pressed our faces up to the lighted window and looked in. Major Variana was talking to a young man behind the counter, and taking off his jacket at the same time. He rested his cane on the counter, and put on a large apron. Then he rolled up his sleeves and went behind the counter where he began making a pyramid of green apples.

" 'It's not possible,' I said.

" 'Are you sure he said he was a Major?' asked Helen.

" 'Yes, of course I'm sure,' I hissed. I looked through the window again, and the Major saw me looking. I thought I was going to die of shame. I hid my face in my hands. Helen said:

" 'He's waving and smiling. He wants us to go in.'

" 'I can't.'

" 'We must,' said Helen, and almost pushed me into the shop. I stood beside the counter and wished I knew how to shrink. Then I heard his voice:

" 'Pinny, dear, how are you? It *is* Pinny, isn't it? And who is this young lady?'

" 'This is Helen, Major. I'm afraid we were rather rude, looking at you like that through the window.'

" 'Not a bit, dear. Natural curiosity.'

" 'Don't you find this shop boring, after all your other adventures?' I asked. The Major fingered his moustache, hesitated. I went on: 'You did have all those adventures, didn't you? They were all true?'

"The Major smiled: 'I have to admit to one lie, one piece of embroidery, of exaggeration, although the answer to your question is, yes, I did really have all those adventures. The thing is, a crocodile has never been within miles of my foot.'

" 'Then what happened?'

" 'I dropped a crate of oranges on it, and broke all the toes. I thought the crocodile story was more exciting. You enjoyed the crocodile story, didn't you, Pinny?'

" 'Oh, yes, I prefer it to oranges . . .' I faltered.

" 'That was the only made-up story, I promise you,' said the Major.

" 'I believe you,' I said, and I did. 'But isn't it dreadfully dull for you now, selling vegetables all day? You can't have any more adventures.'

" 'Not a bit of it, Pinny, not a bit of it.' The Major chuckled. 'This life is full of dramas, I assure you. Why I'd rather face twenty Bengal tigers in a temper than deal with Mrs Sagegrouse in a complaining mood. I see life here, Pinny, and besides, I'm too old for wars now. No army would have me, I fear.'

" 'Is it your shop,' asked Helen.

" 'No, but I am Chief Assistant,' said Major Variana proudly.

" 'You never come walking round the square any more,' I said.

" 'The summer is our busiest time, Pinny. I shall resume my walks now the autumn is here and call on your mother and yourself sometimes if I may.'

" 'Yes, please,' I said, 'and you can tell us more adventures. My mother said you should write a book about them.'

" 'Ah, no, my talent is for having adventures, not for writing about them.'

" 'But you've stopped having them,' I protested.

" 'What a thing to say! Isn't it a splendid adventure, you girls following me (yes, I noticed you!) through the dusk? I'm very glad you did, but you must go home now, or your mothers will be worried. I shall arrange for a carriage.'

"For a moment I half expected him to turn a pumpkin into a golden coach, like Cinderella's Fairy Godmother, but he simply called out: 'Charlie!' in a loud voice, and the young man we had seen through the window appeared from an inner room. The Major told Charlie where we lived, and then filled some paper bags with apples and oranges for us to take home. We said goodbye to the Major, and climbed into a little horse-drawn delivery cart. Charlie sat in front, and the horse, Nutmeg, clipped and clopped through the lamplight all the way to Helen's house. She waved to me from her door. Nutmeg turned towards the square.

"My mother was very angry with me.

" 'I was frantic, Pinny. Do you know it is nearly seven o'clock? Where have you been?'

"I told her about the Major working as a greengrocer, although I left out the bit about the crocodile being made-up. She listened to everything and forgot her crossness a little.

" 'He must be a really happy man. It is a great gift, to be able to find excitement in everything you do.'

"I went to bed that night absolutely determined to be like the Major. The very next day, I asked my mother for a piece of black cloth for my quilt.

" 'Why black, dear?' she asked, and then said, just like you, 'It's such a dull colour.'

" 'To remind me of the Major. To help me find adventures, everywhere.'

"Well, there it is. I don't know about adventures, but certainly a great many things have happened to me during my life, and it is partly thanks to the Major that I can enjoy them all. Good night, my dear."

She switched off the light, and I put my head on to the pillow, and went to sleep.

All the Golden Horses

"'VE FOUND THREE gingham patches, Aunt Pinny. All together in a bunch here."

"Yes, I remember those. Pink and white, brown and white, and blue and white checks. My mother made me three new pinafores for my first holiday in the country."

"Where did you go?" I asked.

"To stay with my mother's second cousin, Jessie. She owned a small cottage, just outside Oxford. I had been ill a great deal during the previous winter and spring, and my mother felt the country air would do me good. We went to stay for four weeks: the last two weeks of August, and the first two weeks in September. I remember that because of the fair. St Giles' Fair in Oxford is always at the beginning of September."

"Did you go? Do you like fairs? Did anything exciting happen?"

"I'll tell you all about it, shall I?" said Aunt Pinny.

"Yes, please," I said. Aunt Pinny put her sewing down on the chest of drawers, and came to sit at the foot of the bed.

"It's nothing to you, I know, to jump into an aeroplane and fly high as a cloud to the other side of the earth. Men have already walked on the moon, and I daresay you, too, will be able to go there one day, although it's not a place that I would enjoy, I feel. When I was small, even a trip in the top deck of an omnibus was exciting, and when I was seven, I had never been on a train, never been pulled along behind a real steam engine. And I had never been to the country.

" 'It's not the proper country, Pinny,' my mother warned me. 'Oxford is a large town, and quite near. Cousin Jessie doesn't live on a farm, you know.'

"Still, and in spite of all my mother's talk, I had a picture in my head of what the country was like: milkmaids in mob caps and farmers in knee-breeches, small houses with roses growing round the doors, stiles, carthorses, shepherds coming down from the hills at sunset, wooden bridges curving over brooks. For a week before we left London, I packed and repacked my case. The three pinafores were ready, with frills running over the shoulders, and round the hem. They had big, deep pockets. Perhaps Cousin Jessie would give me a wicker basket, and I could collect eggs from the henhouse for tea. Brown eggs. I could see it all.

" 'Cousin Jessie doesn't keep hens, dear,' said my mother, when I asked her. That did not really worry me. The image of myself in a frilled, gingham pinafore with a basket of brown eggs over my arm was stronger than the truth.

"We left from Paddington Station. The steam hissed from the engines and stung my nostrils and my eyes. Puffs of blue smoke rose into the iron and glass roof, the highest roof that I had ever seen. In our compartment we put our cases into a luggage rack that was like a fishing net on a wooden frame, and did not seem strong enough to take the weight of all the baggage. All the way to Oxford I worried about it. I was sure it was going to break. When the train started, I listened to the metal clacking of the wheels, and the huffing of the steam. We could see the backs of houses from the window. They looked too small to belong to real people. Children

86

in the little squares of back gardens waved at the train as it went by, and I waved back. Then we left London behind, and fields and green hedges and bushy trees slid past. I even saw real cows, although they, too, looked smaller than I had imagined. In the compartment there were yellowing photographs of buildings with tall towers, and two spotted brown mirrors. Just before we arrived in Oxford, the ladies looked into the mirrors, and patted their hats, and put down their veils, and the gentlemen lifted all the cases out of the nets, which had held firm, after all.

" 'I'll look out, dear, and see if I can see Jessie,' said my mother, and I looked out of the window, too, even though I had never seen Cousin Jessie before. She would, I thought, be a comfortable-looking person in a bonnet, with a lace shawl around her shoulders, and an apron over her skirt. Her cheeks would be pink, of course, from the country air.

" 'There she is,' said my mother, and fluttered a handkerchief out of the window. I could see nobody on the platform like the picture-book farmer's wife I had imagined. I followed my mother to the barrier, and Cousin Jessie was waiting there. As I kissed her politely, I thought: 'She's just like an ordinary London person.' She was not ordinary at all, however. She was the tallest lady I had ever seen, with sad eyes and cheeks as pale as paper, that felt papery when I kissed her. She wore a black hat, and a black cotton dress, and her hands were bony in black lace gloves. I didn't think I liked her very much, except for her voice. When she spoke, I wished she would never stop. Her voice was like a lullaby.

"We drove to the cottage in a pony and trap. I was a little upset to discover that they were borrowed from a neighbour for the occasion, but I felt I was in the country already, trotting in the sun through the wide, tree-studded streets of Oxford.

"The cottage was a disappointment. It was one of a terrace of small, grey stone houses with front doors opening straight on to the road. There were no roses anywhere. There were no front gardens, just a row of brown-painted doors, one after the other. On the other side of the road was another row of houses, just the same, and at the end of the road I could see a patch of grass. There were two benches on the grass, and a duckpond with some ducks swimming around it, half-heartedly.

" 'That's the village green,' said Cousin Jessie. 'Over beyond the pond is the shop, and the local inn, the Golden Lion.' She opened the cottage door, and we went down two steps into a shady room with a floor made out of big squares of butter-yellow stone. It was cool, and it took a little while for my eyes to grow used to the dim light after the glare outside. Cousin Jessie did not believe in a great deal of furniture. There was an upright piano against one wall, a rocking chair, and two hard chairs with rush seats. In the fireplace stood a brown jar full of wild flowers whose names I did not know.

" 'I like these silvery ones,' I said, touching the flat, almost transparent discs.

" 'Honesty they're called,' said Cousin Jessie.

"The only other rooms downstairs were the kitchen and larder. A large, square table sat under the window. A black stove, a stone sink, and a cupboard full of pots and pans and cups and saucers were the only other things in the room. I looked out of the window.

" 'There's a garden!' I said. 'May I go and see?'

" 'Yes, dear,' said my mother, and Cousin Jessie said:

" 'That little shed at the end of the garden path is the lavatory. You'll have your baths in the kitchen here, in that big tub.' She pointed to a tin bath I had not noticed before, on the floor of the larder.

"The garden was a long strip of grass, cut into two by a flagstone path. All along the fence that divided Cousin Jessie's garden from the one next door, the sunflowers grew, a forest of giants, twice as tall as I was, with loose, golden petals, dark brown centres the size of plates, and jungle-thick leaves. I did not know flowers could grow so tall. It didn't seem right. They were alive in a way that small flowers were not, nodding in the breeze, each one staring at me out of its single, furry eye. I wished Cousin Jessie grew roses, like everyone else. I hurried indoors again.

"My mother and I were to share a room. On that first night, I went to bed as the light was fading, and lay for a long time staring at the white walls and the unfamiliar shapes of chair and cupboard. A pale ribbon of light from the lamp downstairs crept under the door and made shadows I didn't like. I looked out of the window. The sunflowers were asleep, petals hanging down, and stems bending over. I jumped back into bed and buried my face in the pillow.

"At breakfast, Cousin Jessie said: 'I hope you won't be bored, Pinny. There's not a great deal to do here.'

" 'Are there no children?' I asked.

" 'Yes, I suppose so,' Cousin Jessie frowned. 'But I don't know them very well. They seem loud and boisterous, and they are never very . . .' Her voice faded away.

" 'Very what?'

" 'Well, very friendly. They seem, I know it's ridiculous, but they seem . . . nervous of me.'

"I looked at Cousin Jessie and understood exactly how the unknown children must feel. She was too tall, and too thin and too pale. I was, I think, a little frightened of her myself. My mother said:

" 'Pinny will go to the shop for you, Jessie. Won't you, dear?'

" 'Oh, yes.' I was pleased. I liked shopping. 'May I go alone?'

" 'Yes, it's only just across the Green,' said Cousin Jessie. 'I shall give you a list, and some money, and the basket.'

"I walked across the Green with a basket over my arm, and pretended it was full of eggs. A boy and a girl, both bigger than me, were sitting beside the duckpond, tearing blades of grass in half. They looked at me and giggled. The boy did have knee-breeches on, but the girl was not a milkmaid. She was wearing a pinafore over her dress, just like me, and her long hair blew about in the sunshine. I could feel them looking at my back, and my plaits seemed tight and prim to me. Their laughter followed me as I walked round the pond.

"The shop smelled of bacon, candles, tea, paper and glue. One side of it was a Post Office, fenced off behind wire mesh. The food part of the shop was on the other side. 'Can I help you, miss?' The lady at the counter was smiling from behind a mountain of butter.

" 'Yes, please,' I said, and I told her what I needed. As she padded round the shop finding eggs and tea, slicing bacon, scooping balls of butter from the shining yellow slopes on the counter, she talked. She asked questions, too, and answered them herself.

" 'You're the London child, of course you are. Skinny and pale. This butter'll soon see the roses back in your cheeks. Jessie Fraser is some kind of relation, isn't that the truth of it? A cousin, that's it. Just what she needs, a bit of company. Been alone too long, that's what's wrong. Shut up inside herself. Won't share her troubles. Nothing else wrong at all, though I do know what they say. No more music now, not like in the old days. Not since He died. She was quite happy before, mind, but not since He died. Garden gone to rack and ruin. Nothing but those sunflowers. Too big, they are. Not natural. Young person'll be very good for her.' The door of the shop opened, and the two children from the duckpond came in,

90

and sat down on sacks of flour beside the counter. They looked at me.

" 'What's your name?' said the boy.

" 'Pinny.'

" 'That's stupid,' he said, and they started laughing and clutching each other, and pointing at me. The lady behind the counter hit them gently on the head with a wooden spoon.

" 'Now, Miles, now Kate, manners. This is Mrs Fraser's cousin from London. Yokels, she'll think you are. Mind you behave now.' The boy leaped off the flour sack and held out his hand.

" 'Sorry,' he said, 'we didn't know you were all the way from London. I'm Miles, and this is Kate, my sister. She's a bit silly sometimes.' He hopped about on one foot, rubbing his other shin where Kate had just kicked him.

" 'Hurry up and finish in here, and then come and tell us all about London,' said Kate. 'We'll wait for you by the duckpond. Don't be long.'

"I told them all about London. They listened with their mouths hanging open. They had never been further than Oxford. Then they told me about the village and the countryside.

" 'I must go now,' I said at last. 'It's nearly lunchtime.'

" 'Back you go then, to the Haunted House. Beware,' said Miles.

" 'What Haunted House?' My voice wobbled a little.

" 'Mrs Fraser's. It's haunted. By her husband. He died ages ago, but he RETURNS.'

" 'I didn't see him last night,' I muttered.

" 'Well, it stands to reason you wouldn't see him,' said Kate. 'You'll hear him. He used to play the piano, and some nights he comes back and plays again: ghostly, ghastly music. You listen tonight.' She groaned, and Miles rattled imaginary chains. Then they began to giggle, and Kate chewed a strand of her own hair.

91

" 'I don't believe you. So there,' I said. 'And I'm going. Goodbye.'

"They were still laughing. As I walked away, Kate shouted after me:

" 'Come tomorrow, and we'll climb the big elm.'

"That night, I stayed awake as long as I could, and heard nothing. We climbed the elm the next day, and Miles and Kate took me to their house for tea. It was the last cottage on Cousin Jessie's side of the road. It seemed smaller than Cousin Jessie's. Mrs Armitage, the children's mother, and their thick-set father who smoked a pipe, Miles and Kate with their wide smiles and flying hair filled the rooms with their movement and talk. We ate bread out of the oven, and homemade jam. Kate said:

" 'No music yet?'

" 'No,' I said.

" 'You wait,' said Miles. 'You wait and see.'

" 'I don't believe it,' I said.

" 'Well, you've got to admit she's odd, your cousin,' said Kate.

" 'Enough of that, girl,' said Mrs Armitage, lifting the cosy from the brown teapot. 'She's a widow. She misses her husband. Nothing odd about that. It's all nonsense, this music lark, I've told you often enough. Now, hold your tongues, both of you, or you'll be scaring young Pinny.' Miles and Kate looked serious. Miles said quietly:

" 'It's true, Mother. We've heard it, haven't we, Kate?' Kate put down her teacup, and looked at her mother.

" 'Yes, we have. It's the truth, Mother.' Mrs Armitage put the cosy back on to the teapot.

" 'Change the subject, children,' she said, and looked strangely at them. 'You'll all be having nightmares tonight.'

"That night, I could not sleep. My mother lay in the bed next to mine, and it made me feel happier to see the shape of her in the moonlight. I strained my ears, hearing creaks and groans in the furniture that I had never heard before. After a long time, I began to drift into sleep. At first I thought I was dreaming, but I woke up, and sat upright in bed, and I could still hear it. Music. Piano music, played very softly, picked out with one finger. I listened to the tune, a thin, pretty waltz, and then I could bear it no longer. I shook my mother.

" 'Mama, can you hear it? The music? They were right. It's a ghost.'

" 'What? What are you doing, Pinny? Have you had a bad dream?' My mother was awake in a moment, hugging me. I told her about the ghost of Cousin Jessie's husband. Then I said:

" 'Listen, you'll hear it.' There was nothing in the silence except the night noises of the house.

" 'Pinny, you must go to sleep. Believe me, it was a dream,' said my mother.

" 'It wasn't a dream. It was the ghost of Mr Fraser.'

" 'Don't be a little goose. Clarence was a very gifted pianist. You said the music you heard was picked out with one finger. Surely a musical ghost could manage a few chords?'

"I laughed at that, and closed my eyes at last, with my mother holding my hand across the space between the beds.

"Miles and Kate were thrilled when I told them the next morning that I had really heard the music. They tried to persuade me to go down to the front room if I heard it again, to see if I could catch a glimpse of the ghost.

" 'Never,' I said. 'I'd never do that. I'd die of fright.'

" 'Cowardy custard,' Kate said.

" 'Shut up, Kate,' said Miles. 'You know you'd never dare, either.'

" 'Neither would you, so there,' said Kate, and for a while they rolled around on the grass, pushing handfuls of it into each other's mouths, and laughing and laughing.

" 'Stop! Pax!' Miles yelled. 'You're right, I wouldn't dare either. But Pinny, you're to listen again, and report anything you hear or see. It would be interesting to know if your cousin Jessie hears it.'

"I heard the music again that night. Again, the waltz was played falteringly three times, and after that I only heard the silence. In the morning, I went downstairs early and found Cousin Jessie pushing some sheet music into the piano stool. She seemed surprised to see me.

" 'Goodness, Pinny, you're up very early. I was just tidying up.' She laughed, although she had not said anything funny.

" 'Do you play the piano?' I asked.

" 'Oh no, no, I don't. Not at all.' Cousin Jessie looked away. 'Clarence, my late husband, used to play a great deal, but now the piano is . . .' she paused '. . . still.'

"I thought of Miles and Kate and said:

" 'Do you ever hear the piano in the middle of the night?'

"Again Cousin Jessie laughed, although this time I had not said anything funny.

" 'The piano? In the night? You must have been dreaming. Who would play the piano now? I must make the breakfast.'

"That afternoon, Miles, Kate and I went walking in the fields.

" 'She must hear it,' said Miles.

" 'Maybe she's asleep,' said Kate.

"We ran races to the far hedge, and forgot about the music in the clear light.

"I did not hear the waltz in the night after that day. A few days later it was difficult to believe that I had ever heard it. Miles and

94

Kate hardly mentioned it any more. We were busy through the long, sunshiny days, in the fields around the village, fishing in the brooks with nets on the end of long rods, paddling with our socks off and our clothes rolled up, running, climbing and lying in the high grass looking up and up at the towering green spears.

"Then we began to look forward to the fair. St Giles' Fair, said Miles and Kate, was the most splendid, exciting, glorious Fair in the whole world, and we were going to it in three days, in two days, in one more day.

"The day came. The three of us travelled to the Fair with my mother and Cousin Jessie in the pony and trap. We were still quite far away when we heard the sound of the steam organs. When we arrived, I was overwhelmed. The whole street was full of tents and booths. The music of the roundabouts drowned the shouts of children. The helter-skelter slide; and the toffee apples, the Wild Man of Borneo, the Amazing Reptile Pit, the Incredible Madame Zara Your Fortune Told for One Penny—we did not know where to go first. Even Cousin Jessie looked happy. She had pinned a cluster of artificial cherries to the brim of her black hat. Miles and Kate and I tried everything. Kate won a prize for shooting: a little goldfish in a bowl. Madame Zara told Miles he would travel far away, which pleased him. I ate three toffee apples and wasted most of my pennies trying to throw a hoop around a brush and comb set which looked as though it were made of silver. Miles said suddenly:

" 'We haven't been on that,' and pointed towards a roundabout half-hidden behind the helter-skelter.

" 'Look,' said Kate, 'isn't it the most wonderful one?' We all went up to it, and stood and stared. There were curly, gilded bits all around the top. The horses were frozen in a gallop, snorting through pink-flared nostrils rimmed with gold. Their manes were the colour of fire and carved into wooden dancing flames. A voice from the heart of the roundabout shouted:

" 'Roll up, roll up! All the golden horses are ready for a ride. All the golden horses. Take your seats, boys and girls. All the golden horses are riding off in two minutes. Roll up, roll up for the golden horses!'

"The music started slowly at first, then became faster and faster, mechanical music, galloping up and down music. I did not notice it at first. I clung to the scarlet pole in the middle of my horse's back. I could see Kate's hair floating out behind her, and I heard Miles shouting something. It was only when the music slowed down at the end of the ride and I could see my mother and Cousin Jessie standing in the crowd, that I recognized the tune. It was the very same tune that the ghost had played, although it sounded rich and jangling coming from the roundabout. We dismounted. The golden horses set off again, and we watched them. I whispered to Miles and Kate:

" 'That's the tune. That's what the ghost plays.'

"Miles said: 'We must ask Cousin Jessie about it. I'm sure she knows something. Look at her.' Cousin Jessie was gazing at the whirling horses, and swaying slightly in time to the music.

" 'Do you know the name of this tune?' I said.

" 'It's called "The Roundabout Waltz",' said Cousin Jessie. 'Clarence used to play it. It has words, too.'

" 'Please tell us,' we said. 'We'd love to hear the words.'

"Cousin Jessie began to sing softly:

> 'Ride with me tonight on a swift, golden horse
> Whose black hooves will never touch ground.
> Golden horses will carry you all round the stars,
> As the roundabout music goes round.'

96

" 'You've got a beautiful voice, Mrs Jessie,' said Kate, and Miles added:

" 'I never knew you could sing like that.'

" 'I don't sing very much these days,' said Cousin Jessie.

" 'That's a great pity,' said my mother. 'You should sing.'

"We went home in the starlight. The music of the Fair went round and round and faded away behind us. No one said anything. Then Cousin Jessie, who was holding the reins, said:

" 'I have tried. Really I have. To sing, I mean. But I can't play, and it sounds so thin without the piano. Sometimes, just to remember what it was like, I take out the sheet music and try the tune with one finger. It doesn't sound as it used to. I generally play at night, because I don't want anyone to hear ...' Cousin Jessie smiled ... 'especially not Clarence, wherever his ghost may be.' She looked at me. 'I'm sorry I woke you up, Pinny. I should've confessed at once, shouldn't I, instead of pretending it never happened?'

"Miles, Kate and I began to laugh. Cousin Jessie looked a little shocked. I said:

" 'I'm sorry, Cousin Jessie, we're not laughing at you, only at ourselves.' We told her all about the ghost, and then she laughed too, and so did my mother. We must have woken a good many people in the village, as we rode up to our door.

"Cousin Jessie changed after that night. My mother played the piano a little, and the next afternoon Miles and Kate came to tea, and Cousin Jessie sang us the Roundabout Waltz. Then we all sang together, every tune we could remember. We had an iced cake for tea. Cousin Jessie had made it herself, that morning. She was wearing a mauve dress, instead of a black one, and she had cut three sunflowers and placed them in a vase on the kitchen table. Maybe I hadn't seen them properly in the garden. Perhaps they looked different seen from underneath. They seemed more friendly on the kitchen table: sunnier and more gentle. Their yellow petals shone in the light, and made it brighter. 'They're very pretty, really, aren't they, Cousin Jessie?' I said.

" 'They can be,' said Cousin Jessie, 'in the proper place. The thing is, they're so tall no one ever looks them in the eye, if you see what I mean.'

"Our time in the country went very quickly after that. On the morning we left, Miles and Kate came with me to borrow the pony and trap that would take us to the station in Oxford.

" 'Will you tell us your address in London?' Kate asked. 'If we ever go there, we'll come and see you.' She took a chewed-up pencil stub and a dirty sheet of paper from her pinafore pocket, and I wrote down my address.

" 'We could write letters to one another,' said Miles.

" 'Oh yes. Yes, we will,' I said. Kate took out another sheet of paper and wrote their address down for me.

" 'We've got a present for you,' they said. 'It's at home.' We stopped at their house on the way to Cousin Jessie's, and Kate presented me with a bunch of wilting flowers. Miles gave me half of his nail collection: five fine, straight, silvery nails with grooves curling round the bottom in a spiral, and neat, flat heads.

"Miles and Kate waved to us as we rode off. They went on waving, and so did I, until the pony and trap went over the bridge and turned towards Oxford."

"Did you ever see them again? Did you write to each other?" I asked.

"We wrote a few letters, but gradually the time between the letters grew longer, and the letters themselves shorter until there were no letters left. I never saw Miles and Kate again, and to tell you the truth, I'd half-forgotten them after a year or two. I remembered enough about the fun we'd had, though, to sew three patches into the quilt when I outgrew my pinafores. Cousin Jessie sold the cottage, and became a choirmistress in Ely, and it was only when I was already grown-up that I happened to be in Oxford again and visited the village. Mr and Mrs Armitage were still there, very old and stiff. They hardly remembered who I was. Miles was in the Merchant Navy and Kate was a teacher in Scotland. I remember them both very clearly now that I'm older, and of course, I have the patchwork to remind me."

Aunt Pinny took her sewing from the chest of drawers, and kissed me goodnight.

Captain Tramplemousse's Children

AUNT PINNY SAID: "Captain Tramplemousse was a pirate."

"You're making it up," I said, pulling the quilt around my shoulders. "Pirates in Kensington?"

"Yes," said Aunt Pinny. "It was the summer. I remember it all quite clearly. It started in the Park."

"Tell me the story," I said, and leaned back against the pillows.

"Well, now. Mama and I were walking through the Park. There were so many parasols and sun hats, so many children in rompers and flowered dresses, that I suppose it must have been a sunny day. But I wasn't thinking about the weather. I was cross and bored. Nothing exciting had happened to me, nothing exciting was going to happen. We had been to tea with one of Mama's customers, Lady Mabel Saltbag, who believed that children should be seen and not heard. All afternoon, I had sat on a straight-backed, plush-seated chair, holding a teacup and saucer on my lap. Lady Mabel had a house that reminded me of Aladdin's cave. There were so many secret passages and stairways and baize-covered doors asking to be explored, so many things begging to be touched: stuffed animals under glass bells, pretty china ornaments, at least twenty little boxes sprinkled on tables about the room. When I put out my hand to pick up a heavy paperweight, Lady Mabel raised her eyebrows into her hair, and pulled her long neck up out of her lacy high collar. 'Keep your hands to yourself, gel,' she bellowed in a voice that was far from genteel. I put my hands back in my lap, and Lady Mabel lowered her eyebrows and her neck, and turning to Mama, resumed the conversation in quite another voice. I was also hungry, but was only offered one iced cake, about two inches square. I dared not raise my voice to ask for another. That was why I was sulky and fretful as we walked through the Park. My Mama tried to cheer me up with talk of eggs and toast for tea, but I was not so easily distracted. I wanted something wonderful to happen, something out of the ordinary.

"And then we saw them. A man and two children were walking along the gravel path towards us. 'Mama, look!' I said, pointing. 'It's a pirate!'

" 'Don't point, Pinny dear, it's rude. And there are no pirates in Hyde Park, as you know. The King would never permit it.'

" 'It *is* a pirate,' I muttered angrily. 'Just look.'

"As they came nearer, we both stood and stared. We were not the only ones. I remember that children stopped running about, ladies lowered their parasols, and nannies clung to the handles of perambulators.

"Captain Tramplemousse was at least seven feet tall, and very nearly seven feet broad, too. His hair and beard were red. Naturally, I had seen bearded gentlemen before, gentlemen with tidy little square beards, or sharp, upturning, pointed ones. This, however, was the beardiest beard I've ever seen. Oceans of red-gold waves, billowing and foaming down to the man's waist. His jacket was made of blue velvet with silver buttons, he wore brown knee-breeches, and black shoes with shiny gold buckles. On one shoulder sat a parrot, a real, live parrot, and over his eye was a black patch.

" 'He *is* a pirate,' I said to Mama.

" 'He certainly dresses like one,' said Mama. 'However, it doesn't do to judge by appearances. Besides, pirates rarely have children, in my experience.' Mama spoke as if pirates, as a breed, were among her closest acquaintances.

"The man was so startling that I had hardly noticed the children at his side. One was a boy, and the other a girl. Pale, sad, ill-dressed creatures they were, smaller than I was, with dark hair, and dark eyes, and skins like old ivory. This strange trio passed along the path, the children almost running to keep up with the giant strides of the man. As they walked away, the parrot shrieked: 'Bring back the dragons! Bring back the dragons!' and then they were out of sight behind a clump of trees.

"For the next few days, I thought a great deal about the pirate in the Park, and the children who were with him. I made up stories about them in the evening, while I sewed. Then, one morning, I heard it: the hoarse voice of the parrot, crying: 'Bring back the dragons!' I flew to the door and opened it to look into the square, and there, on our doorstep, were the pirate, the two children and the parrot. I nearly fainted.

" 'Ha! Ha! pretty maid, and who might you be?' roared the man. 'It is a dressmaker I require, and I was told to come here. You're a little young to ply a needle, ain't you? Have I moored at the wrong berth?'

"It took me a moment to understand that he was asking if this was the right house.

" 'No, no, it *is* the right berth. I mean, house, sir. My mama is the dressmaker. Please come in.' And I curtsied, I don't know why. Perhaps because he was so tall. They swept into the front parlour where Mama was already at work. She stood up and said: 'Good morning, sir, and how may I help you? Please sit down.' The pirate looked at the little chairs and frowned. 'I'd best stand, if you don't mind, ma'am, thank you,' he said. 'My name is Tramplemousse, Captain Tramplemousse of the . . . um . . . Merchant Marine. My cousin, Lady Mabel Saltbag, has recommended you as a handy hand with a needle, which is why I've come aboard, as you might say.' He frowned in the direction of the children, and Mama said: 'Pinny, dear, take these two little children to the kitchen and give them each a biscuit and a cup of milk.'

" 'Yes, Mama,' I said, wishing I could stay with her and the Captain.

"I took the boy by one hand, and the girl by the other, and led them to the kitchen. So, I thought, Lady Mabel Saltbag has a cousin who's a pirate.

"I was right. There was a mystery in that house. My ideas danced in circles through my head, but I managed to tell the children to sit down, and to give them milk and biscuits. They had not said a word. I said, very slowly: 'Do—you—understand—English? Speak —English?'

" 'Yes,' said the girl.

" 'Little bit,' said the boy.

" 'Where have you come from?' I asked.

"The children looked at one another, and then at the door. They seemed frightened. The girl said:

" 'From far.'

" 'East,' said the boy.

" 'China?' I suggested helpfully.

" 'No,' said the girl.

" 'The land below the wind,' said the boy.

" 'That's not on my globe,' I said.

" 'Borneo,' said the girl.

" 'Island in the China Sea,' said the boy. I didn't know what to say.

" 'You're a long way from home,' I said, finally.

" 'No home left,' said the girl.

" 'Fallen down the mountain in storm,' said the boy.

" 'Everyone dead,' said the girl.

" 'But not you two,' I said.

" 'Captain Tramplemousse rescue,' said the boy.

" 'Very good man,' said the girl.

" 'Sailed many months on ship,' said the boy.

" 'And now you're here. Do you like London?' I asked politely.

" 'Very nice, many houses,' they said.

" 'Then why do you look so sad?'

" 'Because of the dragons,' they said.

"They told me their story then. It was long and complicated but the main points of it were these: when the children's home was destroyed in the storm, a strange and wonderful thing happened. The dragon pond in their garden was miraculously saved. The waters in it had turned in an instant to green brocade, and the tiny blue dragons that had lived in the pond were trapped forever as patterns in the cloth. Captain Tramplemousse, who was staying with the children's father at the time of the disaster, rescued the children. He also found time to bundle up the dragon brocade, and take it aboard his ship. He was now, the children explained, about to ask my Mama to make it into a tea-gown for Lady Mabel. They were careful to tell me that it was not *only* because they disliked Lady Mabel that they did not wish her to have this tea-gown. It was also because of an ancient verse, that their amah (who was a kind of nanny) had taught them. I remember the verse. It went like this:

107

'Son of dragon, silken-trapped
Dragon-daughter, blue and green
Come to Sabah in the end
Wearing silk, as king and queen.'

"The meaning, they said, was clear. Sabah was another name for Borneo. They were to wear the brocade and return to their native land as king and queen. With milk-whiskers and crumbs on their fingers they looked far from royal, but I quite liked the idea of helping people who would one day be so grand, and I simply loved the idea of Lady Mabel *not* having a brocade tea-gown. So I made them a promise. I was going to smuggle the material out of the house, and meet them early next morning, before breakfast, at the corner of the square. They asked me what I would like in return. I asked for a small piece of brocade for my quilt. It seemed to me they both looked very relieved, as they agreed. Maybe they thought I would ask for money. It would be a long time before they had a great deal of that.

"Captain Tramplemousse stuck his head round the kitchen door, yelling: 'Avast in the galley, me hearties. We must cast off, set sail, in short, leave.' I shook hands with Their Future Majesties of Borneo, and Mama and I saw them to the front door.

"As I lay in bed that night, I thought about the brocade. I should have to steal it from Mama. I hated to think what she would say if she caught me. But, I comforted myself, if she knew the whole story she would agree that the dragons must be returned to their rightful owners. I fell asleep, dreaming of Lady Mabel's vexation at not having a new tea-gown.

"Next morning, early, I crept into the front parlour and found the brocade. Mama had not even taken it out of its wrapping. I cut off a small piece and hid it in a book. The rest I bundled under my arm, then I tiptoed to the door, and opened it. I ran to the corner of the square, and waited for the children. They came just as I was beginning to despair, and I was happy to give them the dragons, and run home to breakfast.

"I waited and waited for Mama to say something, but she never did. She went to see Lady Mabel twice in the next week, and then never went again. I was glad about that. I waited two years, just to be safe, to sew the green brocade into the quilt. That, I thought, was the end of the story. But, just the other day, in the library, I found a dusty volume called *My Memoirs*, by Lady Mabel Saltbag. I took it out, of course. Would you like me to read you a little of it?"

"Yes, please," I said.

"Very well, then, listen. Lady Mabel says:

" 'That summer, we were overjoyed to receive my cousin, Sir Magnus Saltbag, for a short visit. He was always a droll fellow, full of japes and pranks. On this occasion, he arrived in town dressed as a pirate, and calling himself Captain Tramplemousse. He had, moreover, brought with him a parrot, and the two children of his Italian cook, as mischievous a pair of urchins as you could wish to meet. It was they, I feel sure, who made off one day with my brocade curtains from the Blue Room. My dear late husband had brought the brocade back from Borneo, where his uncle was the Governor-General. Imagine my consternation, therefore, when I awoke one morning to find the windows of the Blue Room bare and totally without curtains. I had only just recovered from this shock when the curtains came back. How, I shall never know. The next day, they were in place upon the windows with only a small square of material cut out of one corner.

" 'At about this time, I recall, I also had reason to dismiss my dressmaker. She came to me with a tale of pirates and tea-gowns and disappearing parcels that I never made head nor tail of. I believe it had something to do with Magnus, but I felt it was as well to dispense with the good lady's services. After all, clear-headedness is a quality indispensable in a seamstress. She was such a treasure that I had been keeping her to myself, until that time, but now, of course, I recommended her to all my friends.' "

Aunt Pinny put the book down. "There are the little dragons," she pointed to a pale-green patch in the quilt, alive with silvery-blue creatures. "After all," she said to me as she left the room, "I didn't like Lady Mabel and I fail to see why I should believe her, even now. She was simply embarrassed to have a real pirate for a cousin. I think the children's story was true. I shouldn't be a bit surprised if they are King and Queen of Borneo at this very moment. Goodnight my dear."

Aunt Pinny switched the light off, and closed the door.

Summer Lace
and
River Water

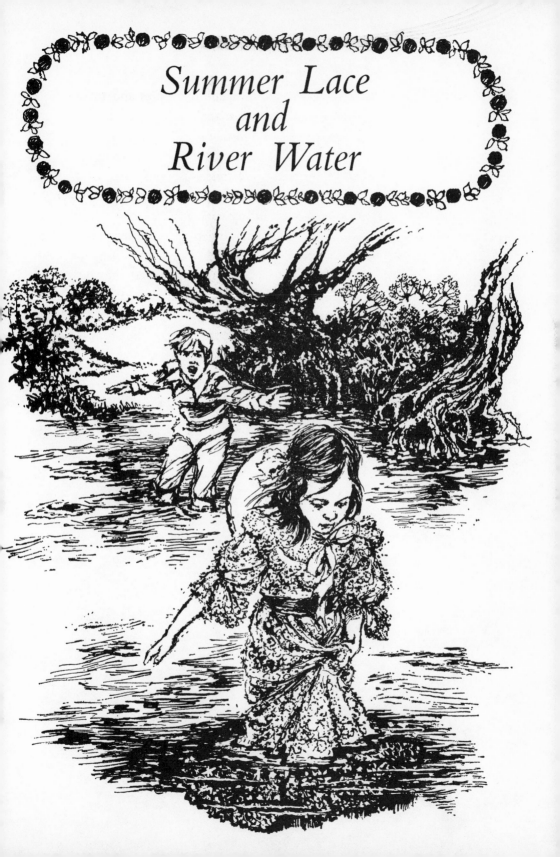

"ONE DAY," AUNT PINNY began, "we were invited to go on a picnic with the Mellquists, who lived in the next street. Mrs Mellquist was a milliner and made extravagant frothy hats to decorate the heads of plaster dummies in the windows of her husband's shop. He was a draper, and my mother used often to go into his shop for a reel of silk or a paper of pins. She became friendly with Mrs Mellquist, who sat in a small room behind the shop, covering brims with yards of net, satin bows or trailing ribbons. They had a little boy, two or three years older than I was, and because Mrs Mellquist and my mother were friends, it was taken for granted that Tom and I were friends as well. The truth, however, was quite different. He was bored with me, and I was a little frightened of him. His eyebrows met across the top of his nose, which made it seem as if he were always frowning. He spoke very little and grunted quite a lot. He had square shoulders and thick legs, and he always wore heavy shoes which clomped alarmingly on the wooden floor of the draper's shop.

"One day, then, my mother said: 'Oh, Pinny, look! How lovely! We are invited on a picnic with the Mellquists tomorrow. By the river. I do hope the weather holds. It will be splendid if it does.'

" 'Where will we go? Tell me all about it. Who else will be

there?' I was six years old, and picnics were a very rare treat indeed. My mother explained. The river sounded wonderful. It almost made up for having to be with Tom Mellquist for the whole afternoon.

" 'I'm going to wear Ruby's lace dress,' I said firmly. My mother slowly stopped thinking about what we were going to pack in the picnic basket, and looked at me.

" 'But that's a dressing-up dress. It's too long. You'll trip up. It'll never do.'

" 'You said that everyone wears pretty clothes. I shan't go if I can't wear it. It's my only pretty dress.'

" 'That's true, I suppose.' She sighed. 'Oh well, I'll hem it quickly on the machine tonight, when you're in bed, and we'll tie a ribbon round the waist for a belt. I daresay it will be all right, but you know, the lace may be stained if you sit on the grass. You will have to sit on a cushion or a rug.'

" 'Oh yes,' I said. 'Yes, I will, really.'

" 'Very well then.' My mother turned towards the pantry. 'Come and help me bake some jam tarts now. We can take them in the biscuit tin.'

"I loved making jam tarts, and I was busy for a long time, stamping circles in the pale, squashy dough with a pastry cutter. My mother put each circle into the baking tin, and then I had a fine time spreading jam all over them, and all over myself, too. My mother chatted to me as we worked. Mr Mellquist, she said, was bringing a camera to photograph us all on the picnic. It would be a long journey to the river. Mrs Mellquist would be wearing a very smart new hat. Did she have time to sew a bunch of artificial cherries on to the side of her straw boater? I was only half listening, because I was already thinking of how I would look exactly like a princess from a fairy-tale in the lace dress. I thought how lucky it was that just the week before, my mother's friend, Ruby, had come to our house with her 'skip'. The 'skip' was a huge, square wickerwork clothes-basket, and because Ruby was a wardrobe-mistress at one of the big London theatres, it was filled with torn, or stained, or simply very old costumes that nobody wanted any more.

"Ruby said: 'I thought these would do for you, young Pinny, for dressing up in. I've been collecting these bits and pieces for years. I've forgotten half the things that are in here, but I hope they'll come in useful.'

" 'Oh yes!' I could hardly answer. As Ruby lifted the lid, I could see swirls and tangles of sequined taffeta, and satin, and old, old velvet with the nap worn away, and I thought I was the luckiest girl in the world. 'Thank you, darling Ruby,' I said, after dipping my arms into the sea of jewel-coloured cloth, 'I can be everything now.'

"My mother found a large box, and we emptied all the garments into it, so that Ruby could take the skip back to the theatre.

"I found the dress after Ruby had left. I could see at once that it was different. It was a very old-fashioned dress, but it was clean, and seemed new, and was not torn anywhere. It was made of cream-coloured lace falling over cream-coloured silk in a filigree of flowers, and spaces and more flowers, cobweb-thin, delicate and perfectly beautiful. I wore it, even though it fell a long way past my feet, and the bodice had to be pinned to fit me. I felt strange in the dress. I did not feel as if I were pretending: dressing up as someone else. I truly felt in that dress as if I *were* someone else, but I did not know who I was supposed to be, nor how I was supposed to behave. It seemed to me more as if I did not fit the dress, rather than that the dress did not fit me. I knew that my mother would alter it to suit me, and I was pleased, thinking that maybe if it were the right size, it would seem more like *my* dress. I would not feel so strange in it, I thought.

"On the morning of the picnic, as my mother put it on and tied a blue ribbon round my waist, she said: 'There, that's better. It looks very pretty now. Much too grand for a picnic, really, but never mind.' It did look better, but it still felt as though it did not belong to me. I put on my sun bonnet and took my soft rabbit downstairs to wait for the Mellquists. My mother had packed the baskets. They stood near the door. One basket was full of food, and the other held cushions, a rug, and my mother's embroidery.

"I can remember very little about the journey. My mother had a glossy bunch of cherries sewn to her hat-band. Mr Mellquist was carrying his camera, and the stand for it, and a cloth to drape over his head while he took photographs. Mrs Mellquist was wearing a green dress, with a mauve and green-trimmed hat of loosely woven straw. The sun shone through the holes in the brim and made patterns of light and shadow on her face. She and Tom were carrying the baskets. Tom had a white shirt on, but he still wore his heavy shoes. A haze clung to the tops of distant trees, and the sky was almost colourless in the shimmering light.

" 'Pinny,' said my mother at last, 'there's the river.' We had been walking through fields for a long time. I was tired already, and the picnic had scarcely begun. But there it was, the river, with a network of sunshine glittering across its surface. The river bank was full of cloudy white flowers, and overhanging willows dabbled their leaves in the water.

" 'This is a good spot,' said Mr Mellquist. We spread cloths, and brought out cushions. My mother took her embroidery frame out of our basket. Mrs Mellquist had a pack of cards in her handbag, and began to play patience on the checkered tablecloth. Mr Mellquist disappeared under his black drapes, and played happily with his camera. I sat on a cushion, with my rabbit on my lap, and wondered what to do. Tom had vanished. I felt quite pleased. Then I saw him walking along the bank towards me. He was smiling.

" 'Where've you been?' I asked.

" 'Up there.'

" 'Why?'

" 'Collecting stones. There aren't any here.' He emptied his pockets on to the grass, and began to build a neat pile of stones.

" 'But what do you want them for?'

"He glanced at me, and laughed. He looked quite pleasant when he laughed. 'Silly,' he said, 'for Ducks and Drakes, of course.'

"I was shocked. 'You're not allowed to throw stones at ducks. It's cruel.' I looked around. 'Anyway, I can't see any ducks, so there.'

"Tom was laughing even harder. He rolled around in the grass and spluttered: 'Not real ducks, silly. It's a game. That's what it's called.'

" 'Show me,' I said.

" 'All right. Look.' He took a flattish stone from the top of the pile and threw it into the river. It hit the surface of the water, then bounced away and hit the water again and again, each time breaking the lacy pattern of sunlight into a thousand rings that spread, and merged into one another.

" 'Lovely,' I said. 'Please do it again.'

"He did it again, several times. Then turned to me and said: 'You try now.'

"My stone plopped into the water a few feet from the edge, and sank at once.

117

" 'Don't worry,' said Tom. 'You have to practise a lot. I go to the Serpentine all the time to practise. I've been going for ages.'

"I felt better about my stone. I said: 'You do it some more.'

"He threw all the stones, one after another, until the whole pile had gone.

"I cannot remember the picnic lunch very clearly. The bees hummed around us, and the food tasted different when we were all sitting on our cushions on the grass, under a roof of green leaves and criss-crossed sunbeams. I remember wondering why that should be so. After lunch, Mr Mellquist took some photographs. We all had to sit very still for a long time and stare at the black box, and at Mr Mellquist's legs sticking out from beneath the black covering that reached as far as his waist. After the photographs had been taken, we lay down in the shade. I put my arm over my eyes. I looked at the sky through the lace on the full sleeves of my dress, and it showed blue and gold in the spaces, among the flowers. Summer lace, I thought. Summer lace and river water, sparkling and rushing. I fell asleep.

"Tom woke me up.

" 'Come on,' he said, 'you've been asleep for ages. Let's go and explore.'

"I stood up. Mr and Mrs Mellquist were still asleep, and so was my mother. I hesitated.

" 'It's all right,' said Tom. 'We won't go far. I'll take care of you.' Suddenly, he did not seem at all glum or frightening.

" 'Yes, let's go for a walk,' I said. We set off along the bank, ducking under branches. Tom told me the names of all the flowers.

" 'This is where I found the stones,' he said, as we came to a place where the bank was not so steep. The river here was bouncing and frothing over rocks and pebbles. We could see them striped with sunshine under the bubbling water.

" 'It looks so cool,' I said. 'I wish I hadn't worn this dress. I want to dip my feet.'

" 'Me too,' said Tom. We were silent for a moment. Then 'Why don't we take our shoes and socks off, and paddle our feet?' he said. 'You could tuck your dress into your sash.'

"I only hesitated for a few seconds. Then we pulled off our shoes and socks, and put them tidily on the bank. I think that there was never any feeling so glorious as the cool water on my hot toes. We jumped about, and kicked, and I did not even think about the lace dress being splashed.

" 'I'm going in a little further,' I shouted.

" 'No, Pinny, don't,' cried Tom. 'It may go deep quite suddenly.'

" I was not even listening. I was drunk with the heat, with the water, with the sun-speckled stones under my feet. Something, I do not know what, was telling me, urging me. I walked right into the river. And then, in a second, it was all around me. My feet could feel nothing, and the water was over my shoulders, cold, suddenly, on my hair. I screamed and screamed until my mouth was filled with water. I remember shouting for Tom, and seeing that he was not there, and struggling to throw my arms up, up, to keep myself above the water that was filling my ears, my nose, my mouth, every part of me.

"Later, they told me how Tom had shouted, how Mr Mellquist had run to where we were, and jumped into the water and dragged me out, how I was wrapped up in the tablecloth, and how my mother cried and thought I was drowned. There was thunder in the sky as we went home.

" 'You were very, very naughty, Pinny,' my mother said the

119

next day. 'You could have been drowned. You must never, never go into the water unless I'm with you, until you know how to swim. Whatever got into you?'

" 'I don't know, Mama, truly I don't. I just felt I had to. I don't know why. I had to walk into the river. I'm sorry, and I won't do it again, not ever.'

" 'I'll wash your lace dress today. I don't think any harm will have come to it.'

" 'Thank you, Mama,' I said, but I knew all at once that I would never wear the lace dress again, that I didn't care if I never saw it, that I wished it had been spoilt and could be thrown away.

"That afternoon, the Mellquists called to see how I was. Tom had brought some pebbles for me.

" 'To keep,' he said. I was very pleased.

" 'If you like, you can come to the Serpentine with me and practise Ducks and Drakes.'

" 'I'd like that,' I said. We could not think of anything to talk about after that, and sat fingering the stones while the grown-ups drank tea.

"A few days later, my mother came back from a visit to the Mellquists' shop and showed me a photograph. There we were, sepia-coloured, sitting forever on the rugs and cushions in the shade of a tree. My mother, Tom and Mrs Mellquist were smiling. Tom's hand was over his eyes, shading them from the sun. I was right in the foreground of the photograph.

" 'You look very solemn,' said my mother. 'But the dress looks lovely. You can see every detail of the lace, can't you?'

" 'Yes.' To me it seemed as if I was looking at the camera with fear. It was odd. I did not remember feeling frightened while the photograph was being taken. I felt very scared in the river, but surely the camera could not show what was *going* to happen? If I had been afraid at the moment the photograph was taken, what was I afraid of? Nearly drowning in the water was the only frightening thing that had happened on the picnic. I felt puzzled, but I gave the photograph back to mother, and tried to put the whole episode out of my mind. That should have been the end of the story, but it was not."

Aunt Pinny sighed: "Look at the lace in the quilt. It looks pretty enough, still, doesn't it? Even on cream silk. I should really have sewn it on to some dark cotton to show up the pattern more clearly."

I sat up in bed: "Why was it not the end of the story? Do tell me the rest. What happened then?"

"The second part of the story," said Aunt Pinny, "took place the following week. Ruby had brought a mountain of mending home with her from the theatre, and my mother had offered to help her. I was happy to be going to visit Ruby, who lived in two small rooms filled with things to look at: posters for old plays, coloured pictures of dancers and ladies with shiny teeth and feathers in their hair. She had a swing mirror on her dressing-table, hung with beads like sweets—big, and round, and pearly-bright. Also on the dressing-table were glass pots full of flower-scented creams, bottles of cologne and a pink swansdown puff in a bowl of face-powder. I used to sit at the dressing-table and cover my face with everything, and hang all the necklaces round my neck at the same time. Then I would take a fan from the Junk Drawer, as Ruby called it. My favourite had black sticks (three were missing) and pink ostrich feathers that blew about like seaweed under water when I shook them. I would then go into the other room to listen to the ladies talking, and pretend to be a lady myself.

"On this occasion, Ruby was darning a sock when I went in.

" 'My,' she said, 'look at Lady Elegant! Come and sit next to me, your Ladyship-lovey.' And she smiled at me with her dark red lips and pushed a yellow curl behind her ear and patted her hair. 'Smartening myself up for you,' she explained. 'Let's hear all the Court gossip, then.'

"She would have played the game quite seriously, I knew, but I felt shy of continuing. I rushed to her lap, giggling, saying: 'No, no Ruby, it's me, Pinny. It's not Lady Elegant.'

" 'Go on with you, your Ladyship. Pinny never wears beads and pink feathers. You're pulling my leg, that you are.'

" 'No, really, look Ruby. It's me. Look!'

" 'Why, bless you, so it is. Well, you fooled me then, and no mistake. Just fancy, Pinny so smart.'

" 'She looked very smart indeed last week,' said my mother. 'I altered the lace dress for her. The one that we found in your skip, you know. For a picnic with the Mellquists. Look, Mr Mellquist took a photograph.' My mother felt in her handbag and said: 'Pass this to Ruby, dear,' and handed the photograph to me. I peeped down at it as I took it across to Ruby. It was full of summer. Last time I saw it, I had not noticed the trellis of sun and shade that the leaves made on the tablecloth. There was Mrs Mellquist's gauzy hat. I could even see a little bit of the river. It was a beautiful photograph, and I spoilt it, staring at the world as if I had seen a ghost. I gave it to Ruby. She looked at it quickly, and then more carefully.

" 'Bless me,' she said, and then again: 'Bless me.' She frowned. 'Well, now, *that* dress. I'd been wondering about it. In the skip, you say? It was an unlucky dress for me and no mistake. It's a very strange thing.'

" 'What's strange?' I asked.

" 'Let me show you something,' Ruby answered, and went to

the sideboard. She came back carrying a photograph album, and began to turn the pages slowly. 'I've found it. Come and see, Ellen. And you, Pinny.'

"We looked. Ruby had placed our photograph next to another in her album, and even though Ruby's photograph was darker and smaller, my mother and I both gasped. The picture in the album was taken a long time ago, but it also showed a picnic, and it could have been our picnic last week. There in the front, I noticed especially, was a frightened-looking girl in my lace dress, or one very like it.

" 'Who's that?' I pointed.

" 'Me,' said Ruby, 'in that lace dress. After that picnic I never wanted to wear it again.' Ruby looked sad. My mother, as if to change the subject, said:

" 'Pinny had an adventure on the picnic. A very lucky escape from drowning.'

"Ruby turned pale, and her fingers shook as she put the photograph album back in the sideboard.

" 'Uncanny, that's what it is,' she muttered.

" 'What is uncanny about it?' said my mother. 'Simply two rather similar pictures of picnics, one with you in the lace dress, and the other with Pinny wearing it. I really think you're being melodramatic, Ruby.'

" 'That's as may be. I shall tell you the whole story and you can decide for yourselves.'

"I settled down happily on the sofa to listen. Ruby went on. 'But first, you must promise me one thing. Never wear that lace dress again. Burn it; or make it into curtains.'

" 'But what a waste!' said my mother.

" 'You must,' said Ruby, 'or I shall not tell the story.'

" 'Very well,' said my mother, 'although I really don't see why ...' "

123

" 'You will,' said Ruby. She took a deep breath and began to speak: 'There was one other person on that picnic. Someone who is not in the photograph.'

" 'Who?' I whispered.

" 'My friend May.' Ruby sighed, and wiped away a tear. 'We'd all gone down to the river together. Uncle Teddy had the camera. Everyone was in pretty dresses. Our hats were lovely. Mine had blue ribbons tied round it. The men wore white trousers. We had a red and white checked tablecloth.'

" 'So did we, didn't we, Mama?'

" 'Yes, dear,' said my mother. 'Be quiet and listen.'

" 'It was a very hot day,' Ruby continued. 'The river looked so fresh. We had all decided to paddle after lunch. But Uncle Teddy said: "Photographs first," so we posed on the grass, under the tree. No one could find May. We sat still for the camera for years and years, it seemed to me. As I sat there (I can remember this clear as clear, mind, and it was many, many years ago), I knew, something told me, it came out of nowhere, that May was in danger. I felt cold in the sun and I knew I should have said something, but we were posed, and Uncle Teddy would have been so cross if his picture had been spoiled. So I waited, and felt fear running up and down my back. As soon as we were allowed to move again, I said: "Where's May? Let's go and look for May." We ran along the bank for a while and then we found her, sinking in the middle of the river.' Ruby stopped and sniffed.

" 'Did she drown?' I said. 'Was she dead?'

" 'No,' said Ruby, 'not dead. But she took a terrible chill, and her health was never the same again. Never the same. I felt so guilty. If I had moved, and ruined the photograph and told the others, we might have found her before she went into the water and lost her footing. The whole day, the whole sunny day, went dark for me. I look at that picture sometimes and think "Ruby, my duck, you were psychic that day, that's what." I could never wear the lace dress again.'

"I spoke slowly: 'I felt funny in the dress, too. I felt as if I didn't know who I was. Maybe I was supposed to be you, Ruby. When I was paddling in the river, something made me want to go in deeper. Was that the dress, do you think, Ruby, thinking I was you, pulling me in to try and rescue May? Was that it?'

" 'Quite likely,' said Ruby. 'I'm sure it's a haunted dress, and no good will come of it.'

" 'A haunted dress!' my mother laughed. 'Whatever next? I'm sure it's nothing of the kind.'

" 'Then what is it?' I said.

" 'A series of coincidences,' said my mother.

" 'What's that?'

" 'I mean,' she said to me gently, 'that all those things happened by accident: two picnics, one lace dress on two occasions, two near drownings. It was all just by chance.'

" 'I think Ruby's right and it's haunted,' I said. 'I think we should burn it.'

" 'Very well, dear,' said my mother, who could see that I was a little worried by the idea of a haunted dress. 'We'll burn it tomorrow.'

"I could not resist cutting a small piece for the quilt. My mother was feeding bits of lace into the boiler, where it blossomed into fire, and then turned black and curled up in ashes.

" 'Will it still be haunted, just this tiny piece?' I wanted to know.

" 'No, that's far too small for any ghostliness to settle on,' said my mother.

"I sewed it into the quilt, and here it still is. Over the years, I've almost forgotten the drowning and the haunting, but I do remember the river that day, and the stones skimming across the water. Happy memories last longer than sad ones, I think. Good night, dear."

Aunt Pinny smiled, and pulled the quilt up round my shoulders, as I lay down to sleep. Then she left the room, and went downstairs.

Apricots at Midnight

"It's your last night, tonight," said Aunt Pinny, as she sat down at the foot of my bed, "and I should like you to choose the kind of story you'd like, as a special treat. What shall it be about?"

"Is there a story about a party?" I said, after thinking for a moment. "I love parties."

Aunt Pinny smiled. "Yes, there are many, many party stories, but which one shall I choose? Let me think . . . Ah, yes, I have it. How would you like to go to Mr and Mrs Edward Triptree's Gala Costume Ball? Quite the grandest Ball there's been. Does that sound pleasant?"

"Did you go? When you were little? Were you allowed to go to a grown-up ball? In costume?"

"It's not as simple as that," said Aunt Pinny. "Listen, and you'll hear the whole story from the beginning." She pointed to a red velvet patch on the quilt. "That," she said, "is the lining of a cloak made by my mother for Mr Edward Triptree, who was to attend his own Ball disguised as a highwayman. I first heard about the Ball one evening in early autumn. The light was beginning to fade from the sky, and it was still hanging like veils from the golden trees. I was looking out of the window into the square when a car drew up right beside our steps.

" 'Mama,' I said, 'here's someone in a motor car coming to see us. There's a driver, too, in a dark green suit and hat.'

" 'It can't be for us,' my mother replied. 'We don't know anyone who owns a motor car.' Still, cars were such a novelty in those days that she rose from her chair, I remember, and came to the window to look at it.

" 'Isn't it brightly polished?' I said.

" 'Yes, lovely,' my mother answered. 'And look inside at the leather seats. It's difficult to see, but there is someone in the back. A lady, I think.'

" 'Yes, and covered with rugs, look. The driver is folding them . . .'

" 'The chauffeur, dear,' said my mother. 'That's what gentlemen who drive cars for other people are called.'

" 'Yes, well, he's folded about three tartan rugs.'

" 'It must be someone who feels the cold,' said my mother. At that moment, a lady stepped out of the motor car, and began to come up the steps of our house. She was carrying a large handbag, almost a suitcase, with tapestry sides. She wore a hat heavy with feathers that covered most of her face, and a pale grey fur coat poured down over her dress. She knocked at the door.

" 'Pinny, she's coming here,' cried Mother in a panic.

" 'I told you she was,' I said, while my mother smoothed her hair quickly, and straightened the cushions on the sofa.

" 'I'd better go and answer it, I suppose,' she muttered, flying out of the room, and I heard her voice and a high, clear voice answering her. After a moment or two, they came back into the front parlour. My mother came in first, and held the door open for our guest.

" 'This is my daughter, Penelope, ma'am,' she said, and I think I curtsied.

" 'Indeed,' said the lady, and made a shrugging movement with her shoulders, which caused her fur coat to slither on to the chair.

"Later, after she had gone, I learned that her name was Mrs Edward Triptree, but while she sat there and talked to my mother, I looked at her. She had a beak-like nose and no chin at all. Her eyes were bright and brown. It was an eagle's face under the feather hat. In one month's time, she told my mother, there was to be a Costume Ball at her house.

" 'Mr Triptree,' she said, 'is to go disguised as a highwayman. It is a whim of mine, and I have decided to humour myself. Here,' she dipped into the tapestry bag, 'is brocade for the suit, lace for the ruffles at the wrists of the shirt, and red velvet with which you may line an old opera cloak of mine. That should be quite sufficient.'

" 'Oh, yes,' said my mother, and I could see that she was delighted at the richness of all the material spread at her feet. 'That should look splendid.'

" 'Splendid is something poor Mr Triptree will never look, alas, but luckily it does not matter. I myself am having a gown sent from Paris (Marie Antoinette, you know) and the girls will look sweetly pretty, as usual. How soon, do you think, will you be ready?'

" 'Oh, in a fortnight at the very latest,' said my mother. 'Not longer than that.'

" 'Good, good, most satisfactory. I shall send the chauffeur to collect the garments in two weeks' time, and my husband will try them on. There will then be time for any last-minute alterations.'

" 'Madam, forgive me, but I have to have your husband's measurements,' said my mother. Mrs Triptree's laugh trilled round the room.

" 'Of course, of course, how silly of me! I have them here, written down especially.' She reached an arm into the bag, and brought out a sheet of paper covered with numbers. This she handed to my mother, who said:

" 'Thank you, that will do very well.'

"Our visitor took up her coat, and my mother showed her to the front door. From the window, I saw the chauffeur unfolding the tartan rugs and tucking them around her knees.

"During the next two weeks, it was difficult to go anywhere without hearing talk about the Ball. All the shops hummed and buzzed with excitement. Mr Silvano, the baker, told us how hard he would have to work, making florentines, rum-babas, éclairs with licks of chocolate on top, little cakes iced in rainbow colours, and apple flans the size of wagon wheels.

" 'And the centre piece,' his eyes opened wide. 'What a creation! A fairy castle in royal icing, set in a snowdrift of sugar. Complete with turrets, and pennants flying and a thousand windows at least.'

" 'May I come and see it before it goes?' I begged.

"He smiled. 'Of course, my dear. It will be something to see, I promise you.'

"The butcher was providing whole piglets, which would be roasted with oranges stuck into their mouths. They did not sound very tempting to me.

" 'But that's not all,' he said. 'No, not by a mile. Oh, no. I mean to say, roast pork is ordinary compared to some of the things they're having. The cook told me. Peacock, if you please, with the tail feathers spread. They had to order that from Fortnum and Mason. Salmon in bowls carved out of ice. Have you ever heard the like? A great fuss and to-do, that's what I call it.'

"The Garland sisters, Miss Posy and Miss Rosy, owned a flower shop. Whether their names made them choose that kind of shop, or whether they changed their names to fit in with the flowers, no one ever knew. But they had never been so busy in all their lives. Every time we passed by, they were thinking about new bouquets for the ladies, worrying about the arrival of hot-house flowers for the table, wondering whether there would be enough gardenias to float in all the finger-bowls.

" 'What's a finger-bowl?' I asked my mother.

" 'It's a little bowl, full of water, beside your plate,' she said. 'You dip your fingers into it when they become dirty during the meal.'

" 'What about table napkins? Don't they have those at grand parties?'

" 'Why, yes, dear, of course. After dipping into the finger-bowls, you wipe your hands on the napkin.'

"All the preparations seemed completely enchanting to me.

"In the evenings that followed, I watched my mother at work on the highwayman's suit.

" 'I wish we could go,' I said.

" 'There's no chance of that,' my mother said. 'And anyway, children do not attend grown-up costume Balls.'

" 'Mrs Triptree talked of girls.'

" 'Big girls, I daresay. More like young ladies, I should think. You, my child, will be in your bed and fast asleep while all the festivities are going on.'

" 'I wish I needn't be in my bed.'

" 'Tush, Cinderella, you'll have Costume Parties in plenty when you're older.'

" 'That's not for years and years. I do feel just like Cinderella. If only I had a Fairy Godmother!'

" 'You have, Pinny dear. I shall wave my wand and you'll see, you'll be up those stairs before you know it, and into your bed.'

"Two weeks after Mrs Triptree's first visit, the polished car drove up to our door again, but to our surprise, as we waited at the window, it was Mrs Triptree herself who opened the back door of the car before the chauffeur was out of the driving seat. She ran up the steps to our front door. My mother hastily let her in.

" 'Oh, Mrs Pintle, such a thing! I really must consult with you. A terrible thing has happened.'

" 'Please come in and sit down,' said my mother and led Mrs Triptree to a chair, upon which she flung herself without even taking off her coat.

" 'It's Betsy, you know. She's the maid who does the sewing around the house. Mending linen, darning socks and so forth. Her mother has fallen sick and Betsy must go and look after her, and will not be back in time for the Ball. I am distraught. What am I to do?'

"My mother looked puzzled.

" 'I'm very sorry, Mrs Triptree, to see you so upset, and I would like to help you, but I do not understand. Why is Betsy so important? Surely she may darn and mend linen when she returns?'

" 'Ah,' said Mrs Triptree. 'I see I must explain. At every one of my parties there is a person whose task it is to be always ready with a needle and thread. Ruffles may become separated from cuffs or hems, bunches of flowers may need to be sewn to necklines of dresses, garments may become torn and need some stitches. A person is generally placed in the cloakroom to deal with such emergencies. I really don't know where to turn.'

"My mother looked at me, and smiled. She said, 'I should be glad to help you myself. But I would have to bring my daughter with me, for I cannot leave her alone, and I should hesitate to ask someone to come and sit with her for such a long time. I expect the Ball will last a long time?'

" 'Until dawn, I shouldn't wonder,' said Mrs Triptree. 'Oh, Mrs

Pintle, I can't tell you how grateful I would be. As for your little girl, we shall certainly find a bed for her, never fear. I shall pay you, of course. Could you come after lunch, on the day? There may be last-minute touches, you understand.'

" 'Of course we shall be there. We are both looking forward to it,' said my mother. I do not think I had ever felt so excited in my life. I would see all the preparations, and the house itself, which, I had heard, was like a palace, and perhaps if I was very good, my mother would let me watch the guests arriving in their costumes.

" 'Thank you so much,' said Mrs Triptree, and was nearly out of the house before my mother suddenly said:

" 'The suit! We have forgotten the highwayman's suit.'

"The bird-laugh rang out again, all around the hall. 'Aren't I a scatterbrain? Poor Edward! I'd better have it, I suppose, though he, I know, would have been delighted if I'd forgotten.' She waited while my mother went to fetch the parcel, and then ran into her car, still laughing.

"During the next fortnight, I made quite sure that everyone knew I was going to be at the Ball—well, in the same house as the Ball, at least. At the baker's, I asked Mr Silvano about his fairy castle cake, and he told me all about it.

" 'I shall see it actually on the table in the house, you know,' I said, hoping to myself that this was true. 'We are going to be there for all the preparations.'

" 'Really?' said Mr Silvano. 'You'll have to tell me how it looks, then.'

" 'Oh, I shall,' I said, feeling very proud.

"I also promised the butcher to look out for his sucking piglets, and I told Miss Posy and Miss Rosy that I would notice the flowers most particularly.

" 'You're a lucky girl,' said Miss Posy.

" 'Think of all the beautiful ladies and handsome gentlemen,' sighed Miss Rosy, waltzing a little in between the flower pots that stood about the floor.

" 'The jewels,' said Miss Posy.

" 'The music,' said Miss Rosy.

" 'The food too beautiful to be eaten.'

" 'The lighted candelabras shining on the damask tablecloth.' They both sighed, and began to twist some hothouse roses into a wreath of pink and white.

"On the day of the Ball, we walked to the Triptree's house after lunch.

" 'You are to do exactly as you're told, Pinny,' said my mother, and go to bed just when I say. I shall be too busy to look after you, and I want you to promise me to be good, and not get into mischief while I'm occupied.'

" 'Yes, I will be very good, Mama.' I was wearing an ordinary dress, and felt a little disappointed. I had said to my mother earlier: 'But it's a party.'

"She had said, very patiently, 'I know, dear. However, it is a party to which you for one, and I, for another, are not invited. Therefore I think it's quite unnecessary to wear party clothes.' That was the end of that.

"The Triptree house *was* like a palace. The drive curved in a grey circle up to the great front door, and downstairs there was a hall where two long staircases soared up from a marble floor. A maid took my mother and me into a pleasant room leading off the hall.

" 'This is where you'll work for now, Mrs Pintle. I'll tell the mistress you're here. Please make yourself comfortable. And the little girl, bless her.' She tickled me under the chin and left the room. Mrs Triptree arrived shortly after that, with an armful of last-minute repairs: satin roses to be sewn on shoes, black velvet for the highwayman's mask (which she had forgotten until the night before), maids' caps with ribbons missing, torn aprons, and gloves that needed stitching here and there. My mother settled herself with the sewing and I stood at the door, and watched the vans arrive.

"Everyone was very busy: heels clattered on the marble, and mysterious parcels, boxes, hampers and crates were carried in by an army of maids. A dignified man, the butler, I supposed, directed everything to its rightful place. All at once, I heard someone say: 'Hello,' and I saw that a small, round ball of a man with a lot of greyish-yellow hair and steel-rimmed spectacles was standing beside me.

" 'Hello,' I answered. 'Isn't it wonderful?'

" 'Do you like it?'

" 'Oh, yes,' I said. 'I just wish I could go in there.' I pointed at the room into which most of the parcels seemed to be going.

" 'Really? That's only the food.'

" 'I'd like to see it.'

" 'Come with me then,' he said.

" 'I must tell my mother.'

" 'I shall tell her myself that I'm taking you on a tour of inspection. She won't mind.'

"I was not sure, but my companion was right. My mother said only: 'Don't be a worry, though, Pinny.'

" 'It will be my pleasure,' said the round little man.

"The dining-room was like a picture from a dream. Long tables were placed all round the walls. Crystallized fruits, sticky yellow and green and orange clung together in small bowls. Silver ranks of knives and forks were lined up on parade, flowers trailed between the huge plates of cakes and in among the glasses. Napkins were folded into the shape of water-lilies. The sucking pigs were already stretched out on beds of parsley in long, silver dishes, and in the most important place of all, opposite the door, stood Mr Silvano's cake, the most beautiful cake in the whole world, every tower and window, every flag and staircase, glittering white and perfect. Maids were putting silver candelabra on the tables, and fitting wax-yellow candles into the holders.

" 'It's like a story,' I said finally. 'Like a picture in a story book.'

" 'Give me steak and kidney pudding at the club. That, and a nice bit of Stilton and a small glass of port, that's what I'd like.'

" 'I'd like to eat a little of everything that's here,' I said.

" 'That's because you're still young,' said the man. I was beginning to wonder who he was, and was just about to ask him, when Mrs Triptree swept into the room. Catching sight of my companion she said:

" 'Really! You are supposed to be seeing to the drinks in the cellar. Please go there at once and help Blenks.'

" 'Certainly,' said the man, and to me he whispered: 'I expect we shall see more of one another later.'

" 'Yes,' I said. 'Thank you for showing me all this.' He waved at me and waddled out of the room. Mrs Triptree showed no sign of noticing me, so I watched for a little while longer, before creeping back across the marble hall, to where my mother was working.

"Supper was brought to us. It was very dull. Cold ham and beetroot, and currant cake and tea. I thought of roast peacock while I ate it.

"After supper, my mother took me upstairs, where another maid showed me my little room. All it had in it was a bed, a chest of drawers and a chair. My mother said:

" 'I have to go now, and sit in the upstairs cloakroom until the ladies arrive. I shall take their coats and see if I can help them. Would you like to come and sit with me for a little while?'

" 'Oh, yes, yes,' I squealed with pleasure. 'I want to see the ladies in their costumes.'

" 'Very well, then, put on your nightgown and dressing gown and slippers, and be as quiet as a mouse.'

"I sat in the cloakroom on a stool, half-hidden behind a screen, and watched the ladies as they arrived. Would I ever, I wondered, be like them, powdering myself with perfumed dust, touching my lips with ruby colour in a silver stick, twirling in front of mirrors in silk, and satin and brocade? I thought I would never be so beautiful. There were shepherdesses, and Roman ladies, Cleopatras, Nell Gwyns, fairies, Columbines, Spanish dancers, and two or three Marie Antoinettes, all a great deal prettier than Mrs Triptree.

"At last, my mother said: 'Pinny, darling, it's time for bed now. Can you bear to go?'

" 'Yes Mother,' I said. 'I suppose so. I'll go to sleep now. I've seen so many lovely ladies.' I fell asleep to the sound of violins playing in the ballroom.

"A short time later, it seemed to me, I woke up again. The music was still playing, and floating up the stairs from the marble hall. I could hear voices and laughter. I left my bed, and went to the door. I could see that the light was still on in the room where my mother was sitting. I tiptoed along the corridor, and peeped in. My mother was sleeping in her armchair, with her needle and thread beside her. I left her, and went to the top of the stairs and crouched down in the shadows to watch the bright crowd below. I saw Mr Triptree at once. I knew it was Mr Triptree because I recognized the costume my mother had made. I was admiring the look of the red velvet peeping out from the black folds of the cloak, when I noticed the highwayman waving at me. I waved back, a little nervous about having been seen, but before I could become really worried, he had disappeared. I forgot all about him. I sat there for a long time, but in the end, I began to feel cold and tired, and I went back to my mother's room. She was awake. I closed the door behind me.

" 'Pinny, what *are* you doing? Why aren't you asleep?'

" 'I woke up. I feel a little lonely. May I sit with you for a minute?'

"My mother sighed: 'I suppose so. You can have an early night tomorrow.'

"I snuggled on to her lap. 'Have you ever been to such a grand Ball?' I wanted to know.

" 'Well, no, not as grand as this. But I have been to some very nice parties. Parties become fun because of the people who are there. The grandness doesn't matter nearly so much, you know.'

" 'I know, but isn't it all pretty?'

" 'Pretty? I suppose it is, really. I'm glad you're having fun.'

" 'Oh, I am. It's the most splendid night.'

"Just then, someone knocked at the door.

"Quick, Pinny, it must be one of the ladies wanting some sewing done. Hop on to the stool, and be very quiet.' My mother stood up, and opened the door. Mr Triptree, the highwayman, walked in, followed by two maids, each carrying a tray.

" 'Put them on that table, please,' said Mr Triptree, and I knew the voice at once. It was the short, round man who had shown me the dining-room that afternoon. The maids left the room.

" 'Well, Mrs Pintle,' said Mr Triptree, 'I think my young friend of this afternoon will enjoy all this much more than the grown-ups down there. And you, I daresay, could do with some refreshment.'

" 'Why, thank you, how very kind of you,' my mother said. 'It's really most kind. We shall enjoy it. Pinny, come and say thank you to Mr Triptree.'

"I came out from behind the screen. 'Thank you, sir,' I said. 'It looks lovely, and I'm very hungry suddenly.'

"Mr Triptree took off the mask that covered his spectacles, and the three-cornered hat that covered his hair. 'Suddenly,' he said, 'so am I. Let us eat.'

" 'But should you not be down there among your guests?' said my mother.

" 'No one will miss me. We shall have much more fun up here.'

"Oh, my dear, if only I could list for you all the delightful things piled up on those two trays! Little china baskets where marzipan strawberries and cherries lay in green leaves, slices of pink salmon, with crescent moons of lemon lying beside them, roast pork, roast peacock, cakes decorated with icing-sugar violets, pale asparagus fingers, and brave scarlet circles of tomatoes. Right in the centre of one tray, there was a bowl of fruit: grapes, and tangerines and apricots with plush skins the colour of sunset.

" 'Apricots in October!' said my mother. 'Just fancy!'

" 'Apricots at midnight taste delicious,' said Mr Triptree. 'Pinny, do have one.'

" 'Is it really midnight?' I asked. I had never been up so late before.

" 'Yes, really. This is a midnight feast. Haven't had one for years. Take some smoked salmon. And I stole a peacock feather for you, Pinny. Isn't it fine?'

"My mouth was full, so I just nodded. After we had eaten everything on both trays, Mr Triptree took a pack of cards out of the pocket of his highwayman's suit, and started to perform some magic tricks. I sat beside my mother, and looked, and drank tiny sips from her glass of port.

"After a while, she said: 'Pinny, you really must go back to bed now, till the morning. You've been very lucky, and almost been to the ball yourself.'

" 'Your mother is right, m'dear,' said Mr Triptree. 'It's been a very pleasant party for me, thanks to you. I don't usually have anywhere to run away to on these occasions.'

" 'Thank you,' I said. 'I've had a lovely time, and I think you look very nice in the cloak.'

" 'Really?' Mr Triptree sounded surprised. 'I feel a little foolish. In fact, I think you shall have the cloak as a present. I'm sure I shan't be needing it.' He unfastened it, and hung it around my shoulders. 'There, that looks very pretty. Goodnight, my dear. Goodnight, Mrs Pintle. Thank you for having me.' He waved at us as he left the room.

"The next morning we went home again. The Triptree house looked cold and empty in the rain-grey light of the morning. Only the glowing red velvet of the cloak was left of all the splendour of the night before. In the dining-room, the flowers were turning brown along the edges of their petals, and Mr Silvano's cake was a yellow, crumbling ruin, with all the glorious icing gone.

"My mother shortened the cloak for me, and I wore it to parties for many years. When it became threadbare, I cut it up for the quilt, and there it still is. Well," Aunt Pinny stood up, "you have quite a long journey ahead of you tomorrow, so you must sleep now. I've enjoyed telling you about the Ball. Goodnight, dear."

After Aunt Pinny had gone, I closed my eyes and thought about all the different patches of the quilt and they went round and round in my head like a kaleidoscope of dreams until I fell asleep.